SCAREDY KAT

Stories to Scare the 💩 Out of You

TABLE OF CONTENTS

FUNNY SHIT

(Laugh So Hard You May Shit Yourself)

THE OH SHIT MOMENTS

(Funny AF Life Accidents)

TABLE OF CONTENTS

Public Humiliation

(Witnesses Included)

The Shitheads

(Characters That Should Be Flushed)

TABLE OF CONTENTS

 Stories to Scare the Shit Out of You

Legends & Lore

(Stories passed down... like trauma)

 No Bullshit

(Real Talk from the Author)

Funny Shit
(Laugh So Hard You May Shit Yourself)

Not every situation needs your energy... some just need distance and a closed bathroom door.

ELEPHANT
BALLS

ELEPHANT BALLS

There are moments in life where you realize... You've made a series of very poor decisions. This was one of those moments.

It started off like a normal day. Sun out. Pool day. Good vibes. My buddy—let's call him *Lance*—had just started his "new routine." You know the type: gym twice a day, protein shakes that smell like drywall and suddenly giving advice nobody asked for.

"Bro, I'm optimizing my hormones."

Fast forward. We're sitting poolside, beers in hand, life is good.

Lance casually says:

"Hey... I gotta tell you something, but don't laugh."

Now anytime a man says don't laugh... You already know it's about to be bad.

He leans in. Looks around. Then says:

"So... the other day...

one of my Balls got Bigger."

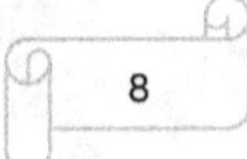

I pause. *"Like... how much bigger?"*

He looks me dead in the eyes: *"Like... noticeably."*

Now I'm interested.

This is no longer casual conversation. This is medical mystery meets bad decisions.

He continues:

"I thought it would go away... but it didn't."

Of course, it didn't.

Because nothing that starts with:

"I thought it would go away..."

...ever goes away.

So, what does Lance do?

Does he go to a doctor immediately?

No. He waits. Because men have a built-in system that goes:

"If I ignore this long enough... it might fix itself."

Spoiler: It did not fix itself.

Eventually, panic sets in.

Because now...

- we're no longer in "minor inconvenience" territory
- we're entering Elephant Balls status

So, he finally goes to the ER. Walks in. Tries to act normal. You know... like a man holding together a situation that is very much falling apart.

Doctor asks:

"What seems to be the problem?"

And Lance says:

"I think... one of my balls is too big."

There is no dignified way to say that. None.

Now he's on a table. Bright lights. Zero privacy. Regret setting in. Doctor takes a look... pauses... and says:

"Yeah... we're gonna need to take care of that."

That's NEVER a comforting sentence. Then comes the part that ended me.

They bring out a needle.

And the doctor says:

"We're just going to relieve the pressure."

Relieve. The. Pressure.

At that moment, Lance said his soul left his body and was watching from the ceiling like:

"This is what we're doing now?"

And just like that... Problem: Solved. Dignity: Gone Forever.

We're back at the pool... and he finishes the story like it's nothing. Takes a sip of his drink. And says: *"Yeah... so I'm good now."*

I just stared at him. Because in that moment... I realized two things:

1. Some people should not be trusted with "optimization"
2. And most importantly...

If your body starts doing something weird...

GO. TO. THE. DOCTOR. EARLY.

Because the longer you wait... the closer you get to: Becoming a circus sideshow freak... and part of a hidden zoo exhibit... **ELEPHANT BALLS**

The Dutch Oven

CC

THE DUTCH OVEN

There are levels to relationships. The cute phase. The honeymoon phase. The "we finish each other's sentences" phase. And then… *There's this.*

It always starts innocent. Late night. Lights off. Both of you in bed. Comfortable. Safe.
Too comfortable.

One of you feels it. That pressure. That little idea. And instead of doing the mature thing…

You choose chaos.

You let it out. Quiet. Strategic. Dangerous.

And then… *You make a decision.*

A terrible decision.

You pull the blanket over their head.

Seal it in. Like a war crime.

Immediate reaction:

"WHAT THE HELL??!"

Thrashing. Kicking. Fighting for oxygen.

Trust? Gone.

And the worst part? You're laughing. Like this is funny. Like this won't come back to haunt you. Because it will. Oh, it will. Maybe not today. Maybe not tomorrow.

But one night… when you least expect it…

The roles reverse. And suddenly…

You're the one trapped.

Gasping. Regretting every decision that led you here.

Because relationships aren't about love.

They're about balance.

And Revenge.

And once the Dutch Oven has been introduced…

There's no going back.

Love is sharing everything…

even things you shouldn't.

Some doors once opened cannot be closed. Especially when The Dutch Oven is introduced.

THE
DUTCH
OVEN

THE PRIZED POOP

THE PRIZED POOP

Every family has a problem. Some are small. Some are manageable. And then… *there's him.*

He was her son. Spoiled. Comfortable. Completely unbothered by life. Gamer by day. Cashier by night. No goals. No ambition. Just vibes…
and apparently… ***A Legacy.***

Every morning… she would walk into the bathroom. And there it was. Waiting. Unflushed. Unapologetic.

Placed like it meant something.

At first, she thought it was laziness.
Then forgetfulness. Then… *pattern.*

Because it wasn't random. It was… *intentional.* He didn't just leave it. He presented it. Positioned perfectly. Centered. Like it was on display.

One morning she asked:

"Why do you keep doing this?"

He didn't even look up. Controller in hand.

"No one appreciates my work."

Work? That's when she noticed something worse.

It wasn't just at home. It followed him. Work bathroom. Friend's house. Public places. Everywhere he went… He left…*a Signature.*

Same placement. Same confidence. Same… *Pride.* Like some people leave their mark on the world…

He literally did. People started talking.

"Have you seen it?"

"It's back again…"

"It's the same one…"

No one knew who.
But everyone knew: It wasn't normal.

Until one day… his mom followed the trail. Watched him. Waited. Caught him. Mid-drop. He looked up. No shame. Just *"…you found me."*

She stood there. Processing. Years of effort. Years of patience. Years of hoping he'd grow up. And finally… she understood.

Some people want to leave a legacy.

Some people… just leave it in the toilet.

Not all masterpieces belong in a museum.

Some people peak early… and leave it behind.

IT'S
BACK
AGAIN!

Skid
Mark

SKID MARK

Marriage is built on love. Trust. Communication.

…and apparently… ***Laundry Trauma.***

THE SITUATION

Every Sunday… Like clockwork… She does the laundry.

Lights. Darks. Delicates.

And then… *his pile.*

At first… She thought it was a one-time thing.

"Maybe he had a bad day…"

"Maybe it was an accident…"

But no. This… was a pattern.

THE DISCOVERY

One pair.

Two pairs.

Three pairs.

Every week… ***Evidence.***

And not subtle. Not faint. **AGGRESSIVE.**

She stands there holding them like:

"What... am I looking at right now?"

THE INTERNAL DIALOGUE

"Is he okay?"

"Does he know?"

"HOW DOES THIS KEEP HAPPENING??"

THE BREAKING POINT

One day… It's worse. She opens the washer… and just stares. Because now it's not just marks…

it's a Crime Scene.

That's when she snaps.

THE PLAN

No yelling. No confrontation. Just… *Strategy.*

She washes them. Folds them. Places them neatly in his drawer. But on top? *A note.*

THE NOTE

You are a grown man. Figure it out.

-Respectfully, your wife.

THE REACTION

Later that night… *He opens the drawer*. He sees the note. *Freezes.* Looks around like someone's watching him. Because deep down… *He KNOWS.*

THE NEXT WEEK

Laundry day comes. She hesitates…

reaches into the pile…

…and pulls out a pair.

Clean. *Another.* Clean. *Another.* **CLEAN.**

THE VICTORY

She doesn't say anything. He doesn't say anything. But something changed. Because sometimes in marriage… you don't need a fight… you just need a note… and a little shame.

Love is Patient. Love is Kind.

But love also says: **"Absolutely not."**

You are a grown man.
Figure it out.
Respectfully, your wife.

★ NO SHIT ★
WHISKEY

NO SHIT

A quiet afternoon. Dust blowing through a small roadside mini mart. The bell above the door rings… In walks a man. Calm. Steady. No nonsense.
He approaches the counter. Looks the cashier dead in the eyes and says: **"I need toilet paper."**

The cashier sighs. Shakes his head.
"Sorry... we're all out of Charmin." Pauses…
Then adds: *"But we do have one roll left..."* He reaches under the counter… Lifts it up like it's something special. **"John Wayne Toilet Paper."**
The man nods. No hesitation. **"I'll take it."**
He pays. Walks out.

THE NEXT DAY

The bell rings again. Same man. Same calm energy.
He walks straight to the counter…
Places the roll down. **"I want a refund."**
The cashier blinks. Confused.
"We don't usually take returns on toilet paper..."
Pauses… Looks at him. *"But... I gotta ask."*
The man leans in slightly. Completely serious.

"It's rough." "It's tough."
"And it doesn't take Shit from Anyone."

OUTPOST
MINI MART
JOHN WAYNE
TOILET PAPER
ROUGH! TOUGH! DON'T
TAKE SHIT FROM ANYONE!
6.39
WE'RE OUT
OF CHARMIN!
ONE ROLL LEFT...
JOHN WAYNE
TOILET PAPER!

TOUGH AS
RAWHIDE
WHISCEY

SH*T HAPPENS

The
Oh Shit Moments
(Funny AF Life Accidents)

OH
SHIT

OH SHIT

He found the coin by accident.

Not shiny.

Not special.

Just... there.

But when he picked it up—

A voice.

"Rub it three times...

and you'll get three wishes."

He laughed.

Then rubbed it anyway.

First wish:

"I want fortune."

Done.

Money everywhere.

Second wish:

“I want fame.”

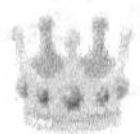

Done.

People knew his name.

He smiled.

Two for two.

Walking down the sidewalk... coin in hand...

Thinking about the third.

What could go wrong?

He rubbed it again. Just like before.

But this time—His foot slipped.

Direct hit. Fresh. Warm. Unavoidable.

He looked down.

Paused.

And without thinking—

He said:

"Oh shit."

The world went quiet.

Too quiet.

Then—

He wasn't standing anymore.

He wasn't breathing.

He wasn't even human.

He was...

Exactly what he said.

Be careful what you wish for...

And more importantly,

Be Careful

where you step.

OH
SHIT

THE
CHEF'S
KISS

THE CHEF'S KISS

She wanted it all. The Life. The House. The Family. The kind of life where everything looked perfect… even when it wasn't.

Newborn baby. Two kids running in circles.

Dogs barking. Cats knocking things over.

Laundry. Dishes. Errands. Carpool.

And somehow… She still made it look easy. Because she was that mom. The one who:

• *Cleaned Everything* • *Remembered Everything*
• *Did Everything*

Even when no one noticed. And today?

Mother's Day. Which somehow meant… more work. Because of course, it did.

"Fresh baked cookies would be nice when I get home."

Of course, they would. Of course.

The day spiraled. Baby crying. Dog threw up. One kid needed help. Another needed something immediately. *The house?* A disaster. *Her brain?* Worse. Then— it hit her. *The cookies.*

She moved fast. Changed a diaper. Grabbed ingredients. Preheated the oven. Chaos everywhere. No time to think. She washed her hands. Quick. Too quick. Because the baby was crying again. And something… *was missed.* Cookies in the oven. House slightly under control. She exhaled.

He walked in. Right on time. He smiled. Saw her. Saw the cookies. Walked up behind her. Soft voice. *"You're amazing, you know that?"*

Then—he noticed it. A little smudge. On her wrist. Chocolate. Of course, it was chocolate. He took her hand. Slow. Playful. Leaning in… *Romantic.* That kind of moment. And then—*He licked it.*

Pause. Complete silence. His face changed. Slowly. Processing. Regret loading…
"…that's not chocolate."

She froze. Looked down. Looked at him.
Looked back at her wrist. Oh. Oh no.
Neither of them spoke. Because there are moments in life… where words don't help.

He walked to the sink. Quietly. Washed his mouth. Twice. And from that day on…

He never asked for fresh baked cookies again.

JUST
SAY
NO

JUST SAY NO

There comes a point in life where you realize… boundaries are necessary. Not optional. Not negotiable. Necessary. *Mine?*

My Bathroom.

Let me be very clear.

This is not:

- a public restroom
- a gas station
- a *"hey can I just real quick"* situation

This is: ***My Sanctuary.***

And yet… People. Keep. Asking.

Friends. Family. Repairmen.

"Hey... can I use your bathroom?"

No.

Not: *"Just a minute"*

"I'll be quick"

"I barely have to go"

No.

Because first of all… it's gross. I already have enough problems in life. Now, I'm supposed to add:

- Butt Germs
- Mystery Splashes
- Pee on the Seat
- AND the possibility of a Full-Blown Situation

Absolutely not.

And don't even get me started on the mental images. Because once you've seen something…
You can't unsee it.

Like the plumber. Bent over. Working under the sink. And suddenly your brain goes:

"What if..."

Nope. We're not finishing that thought.
Because I do not need:

Visions, Trauma or someone casually dropping a Poop Baby in my Sacred Space.

No, thank you. Let me explain something.
My bathroom is not just a room.

It is:

- a Place of Peace
- a Place of Privacy
- a Place where I go to Escape the World

You don't just walk in there with:

Your Chaos, Your Digestive System

and Your Poor Decisions

That's like asking:

"Hey, can I borrow your toothbrush?"

No. And also, what is wrong with you?

For me, letting someone use my bathroom feels like:

Asking the Pope to shower in Holy water.

We don't do that.

So, here's the rule.

Simple. Clean. Non-negotiable.

Go before you come over.

And if you didn't?

Don't come at all.

Because I am not:

- Responsible
- Available
- or Emotionally Equipped

to deal with whatever situation you thought you could handle… but clearly could not.

So, from now on… Let's all be adults.

Keep:

Your Pants Zipped,

Your Body Upright and

Your Underwear in Place

And most importantly… keep your bodily functions away from my house.

Just Say No.

Before it turns into:

A Situation, A Story

Or worse…

A Permanent Memory.

THE
EMPTY
ROLL

THE EMPTY ROLL

There are moments in life that define you.

This was one of them.

He checked his watch. Twenty minutes.

That's all he had before the most important interview of his life. The kind that changes everything.

He chose the worst possible time to use the restroom. Public building. Cold tile. Too quiet.

He sat there, focused, rehearsing answers in his head. Confidence. Eye contact. Firm handshake.

Then— *a voice.*

"Hey... hey man..."

From the next stall.

"Yeah?" he replied, already annoyed.

"...you got any toilet paper?"

He froze. He looked down. Counted. Just enough. Not extra. Not shareable.

"Sorry," he said. "I've got just enough."

A pause. Then—

"C'mon, man... I'm in a bad situation here."

He sighed. Not his problem.

"I can't help you."

The voice changed. More desperate. More real.

"Please. I'll pay you."

He rolled his eyes.

"Twenty bucks."

Silence.

"Fifty."

He stared at the stall wall.

"Hundred dollars."

For a second…he considered it.

Then shook his head. "Not today, man."

A beat. Then, colder: "Use your hand."

Silence again. Longer this time. Then a quiet…

"...okay."

He finished quickly. Got up. Washed his hands.

Didn't look down. Didn't think about it. And left.

The interview room was quiet. Professional. Perfect.

The boss hadn't arrived yet.

He straightened his tie. Rehearsed again.

Then the door opened.

Shoes. That's what he noticed first.

Polished. Expensive.

But familiar. Too familiar.

The man stepped in. Sat down. Smiled.

They didn't look at each other. Not yet.

But they both knew.

Because they both remembered the shoes.

A slow silence filled the room.

Then the man across from him leaned forward…

and extended his hand.

The same hand.

"Let's begin," he said.

BOMBS AWAY

BOMBS AWAY

He hated birds. Not casually. Not "they're annoying." Deep. Personal. Hatred.

Especially crows. Ravens.

"They're bad omens," he'd say.

"Something's wrong with them."

So, growing up... He made it his mission. BB gun in hand. Picking them off. One by one. He thought it was nothing. Just a kid being a kid. But birds? They notice things. They remember. And somewhere... a network formed.

Silent. Watching. Waiting.

It started small. A single drop. On his shoulder. "Whatever." He wiped it off.

Then it happened again. *And again. And again.* Everywhere he went... They were there. *Watching.*

At the beach? Seagulls circled. Closer. Closer. Then— *Impact.*

One. Two. Five. *Like Kamikaze pilots.*

No hesitation. No mercy.

His car? Candy apple red Corvette. Freshly washed. Polished. Perfect. For about... ten seconds.

Direct hit. Center hood.

Then another. Then another. Like they were aiming. Because they were.

Driving range? Mid-swing—Right down the back of his shirt. He froze. Didn't even finish the swing. Just... stood there.

On a date? Of course. Nice restaurant patio. Trying to impress. Telling a story. Then—

Double. Hit.

One on him. One on the table.

Date over. Immediately.

That's when he realized... This wasn't random. This was... organized. Because every time... he looked up... They were there.

Watching. Waiting.

And every time he thought he was safe...

They reminded him.

Because karma...

doesn't always come quietly.

Sometimes...

It comes from above.

You can't outrun what's above you.

The network never forgets.

He used to shoot birds for fun...

Now they never miss.

EMPLOYEES
MUST WASH
HANDS

THE
ACCIDENT

THE ACCIDENT

Post-divorce. Which means:

• *Rebuilding* • *Surviving*

• *Pretending I had everything under control*

I decided to take my kids to Newport Beach.

Fresh Air. Ocean Breeze. A Reset.

It was a good day. The kind of day where you think:

Okay… maybe I'm getting through this.

And then we drove home. Traffic.
Not normal traffic. The kind of traffic where you don't move. At all. ***Brake lights. Endless.***
And then… It hit me. *I had to go.*
Not a *"maybe I can wait"* kind of go.
A RIGHT NOW kind of go. I looked around.
Nowhere to exit. Nowhere to pull over.
Nowhere to run. Just… *Cars.*

So, I did what any rational, composed, fully grown adult would do. I started bargaining with God.

"Please… not today."

"Please… I can hold it." "Please…"

I could not hold it. And there it was.

The Accident. Not a car accident.
A personal one. I took a breath. Looked at my kids.
And said, calmly: ***"I just had an accident."***

They didn't panic. They didn't scream.
They just… *processed.* Because kids? They take your tone. Eventually, traffic moved. And I got off the freeway like my life depended on it.
Fast food bathroom. *Dignity?* Gone. But handled.
Cleaned up. Recovered. Back on the road.
Crisis over. So, I thought.

Later… My ex texts me. Angry. Serious. Accusatory.

"How dare you take the kids and not tell me you were in an accident."

And that's when it clicked. Oh. He did hear about the accident. Just… Not the one he thought.

I didn't respond. Because honestly? How do you even explain that? Some accidents involve cars… and some involve
poor life decisions and bad timing.

Not Every Accident Needs a Police Report.

THE ACCIDENT

POOP
BABY
IT'S A BOY!

POOP BABY

There comes a time in every person's life…

A moment of reckoning.

A battle not fought in public…

but behind a locked bathroom door.

It starts innocently.

You sit down thinking,

"this will be quick."

Oh… how wrong you are.

Minutes pass. Then more minutes.

Then suddenly…

you're sweating

gripping the counter

questioning your life choices

You begin to breathe differently.

Deep Inhale… Slow Exhale…

You don't even realize it…

…but you've entered: **Lamaze Mode**

At this point you're not "using the bathroom" anymore…

You are Delivering Something

Time loses meaning.

Your legs fall asleep.

Your soul leaves your body.

Then…IT HAPPENS.

A moment of silence… *A pause…*

A release so powerful it feels spiritual.

You sit there. Still. Processing.

And then the thought hits you:

"That… was not normal."

You look down…half proud…half concerned…

and whisper: *"Do I… name it?"*

Because after what you just went through…

That wasn't a poop. **That was a Poop Baby.**

You came in one person…

…but you didn't leave alone.

POOP
BABY
IT'S A
BOY!

EXPLODING
DIAPER

BabyWipes

EXPLODING DIAPER

It always starts with confidence.

"He's fine." "She's fine." "It's just a little diaper."

You've done this a thousand times.

Baby looks peaceful. Cute. Innocent. Too innocent. That's your first mistake.

Because then… *You smell it.*
Not normal. Not mild. Something… *catastrophic.*

You go in. Open the diaper. And immediately regret every decision you've ever made. *It's not contained.* ***It's not even CLOSE to contained.***
It has escaped. Up the back. Down the legs. Somehow… defying physics.

"How did it get THERE??"

You pause. Because this isn't just a diaper change anymore. This is a situation.

Wipes? Useless. *Bath?* Mandatory. *Clothes?* Gone.
Your soul? Questioning everything.
And the baby? Smiling. Like nothing happened.
Like they didn't just commit a war crime.
It wasn't a diaper… ***It was a containment failure!***

Every parent learns the same lesson…
Never Trust a Quiet Baby.

EXPLODING
DIAPER

Public Humiliation

(Witnesses Included)

THE
PERFECT
ROUTINE
1

THE PERFECT ROUTINE

I was the kind of girl people assumed belonged. Blonde hair. Neat ponytails. Matching leotards. I looked like I fit in. But I didn't.

The "cool girls" liked me because I looked like them. But I never acted like them.

They whispered. They laughed. They picked people apart like it was part of the routine. I hated that. So, I sat with the other girls. The quiet ones. The awkward ones. The ones who tried hard… and didn't always land it.

My parents didn't like that.
"They're not like you," they'd say.
They were wrong. They were exactly like me.

Competition day wasn't really a competition. It was a show. A "look what you learned" moment for parents.

Everyone lined up. Waiting. Watching. Judging. She was next. One of my friends. Nervous. You could see it in her hands. In the way she shifted her weight.

And then— a voice. A mean girl. Smirking.
Leaning just enough to be heard.

"You're gonna mess it up."

Quiet. Sharp. Just enough to cut.

My friend didn't respond. She stepped forward. Took her place. Breathed in. And went into her cartwheel. That's when it happened.

At first… I didn't understand what I was seeing. Then I did. A spray. A full arc.

Time slowed. The room went silent. And in one perfect, unstoppable moment—It landed.
Right. In. The mean girl's mouth.
Dead center. She didn't even have time to react.

No one moved. No one spoke.
The entire room just… *froze.* Except me. I clapped.
Once. Loud. Because honestly?
It was the best routine of the day.

Some people spend their whole lives trying to be perfect. Trying to fit in. Trying to be liked.

But sometimes, the universe steps in.
And reminds everyone—when to
Shut the Fuck Up.

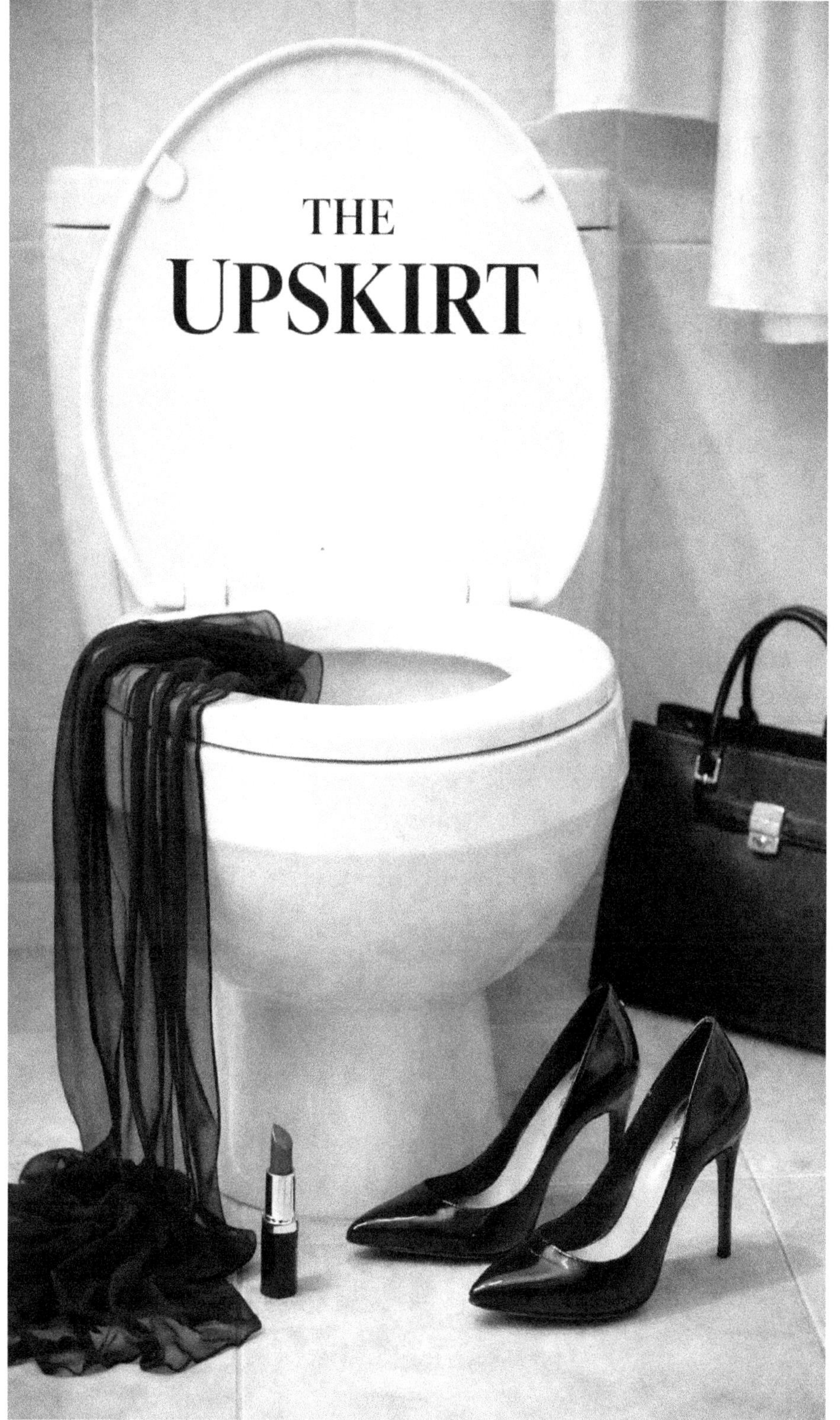
THE
UPSKIRT

THE UPSKIRT

It starts with a rush. Late. Always late.

Bathroom line too long. Time slipping.
Meeting starting. No time to think. Quick fix.

Pantyhose on. Except… No panties. *"It's fine."*
No one will notice. They never do.

Confidence on. Heels on. Game face ready.

You walk out.

Strong. Focused. Professional.

And then… *you feel it.* Something off.

A glance back. Toilet paper. Trailing from your heel.
Crisis. But manageable.
You pivot. Graceful. Strategic.
A perfect little swipe with the other heel—*Gone.*
Like it never happened.

Recovered. Composed. Untouchable.

You enter the meeting. All eyes on you.

Of course, they are.

You think:
I look good today.

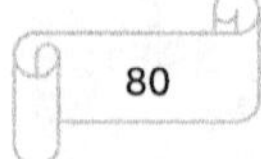

You walk to the front. *Confident. Commanding.*

Turn your back to face the board.
And that's when it happens. Not for you. For them.

Silence. A different kind of silence. Not respect.
Not attention. Processing.

Because what they're seeing...

is not what you think they're seeing.

You're leading. Talking. Pointing at charts.

Full authority. Full confidence.

Completely unaware.

Because your pantyhose? Did their job. *Perfectly.*
Just... *a little too perfectly.*

And from behind? There's no mystery.

No illusion. No protection.

Just... *commitment.*

Ignorance is Bliss.

But a bare ass? It is cold.

Always Double-Check Your Exit.

CENSORED

THE OFFICE
MUNCHER
Elmhurst
1925
UNSWEETENED
ALMOND
MILK

THE OFFICE MUNCHER

Every office has one. You don't see them… but you know they exist. Lunch disappears. Snacks vanish. Leftovers? Gone without a trace. But this time… ***They messed with the wrong person.***

Enter: ***Sally.***

Sally isn't like the others. While everyone else is:

- eating chips
- microwaving mystery pasta
- drinking gas station coffee

Sally?

- ❖ Whole Foods only
- ❖ Organic Everything
- ❖ Labels Read like Sacred Scripture

And her crown jewel…

- ➢ $9 Almond Milk

Not the cheap kind. We're talking:

- ❖ Elmhurst 1925 level elite
- ❖ no gums
- ❖ no fillers
- ❖ just pure, liquid privilege

And someone… ***keeps drinking it.*** Not a sip. Not a splash. THE WHOLE CARTON. Day after day… Sally opens the fridge… Empty. *Again.*

At first, she tries to stay calm.

Deep Breath.

Green Tea.

Manifestation.

But then… ***it happens Again.*** That's when Sally snaps. Because listen… She makes the SAME money as everyone else. She just chooses:

- Discipline
- Health
- $9 Almond Milk

And now some office gremlin is out here:

Living Dairy-Free on HER Dime

THE PLAN

Sally doesn't complain. She doesn't send emails. She doesn't label the carton. No.
She chooses… **Revenge.**

The next morning… She places a fresh, beautiful carton of almond milk in the fridge. Perfect. Untouched. Inviting. But inside? 💀 **LAXATIVES.** Not a little. Not a hint. A life-altering amount.

Then Sally waits.

THE STAKEOUT

The office is quiet. People typing. Phones ringing. Karen complaining. And then… From the distance… A sound. A chair scraping.

A sudden pause. Then… *RUNNING.*

Fast. Urgent. Desperate. Followed by: *Bathroom Door **SLAM***, then Silence. Then… another door slam. Because one bathroom? Wasn't enough.

THE REALIZATION

Everyone in the office freezes. Looks at each other. And then someone whispers: *"Oh my God…"*

Sally? Sips her tea. Unbothered. At peace. Because justice… has been served. If you're going to steal someone's lunch… At least make sure…

It's not Sally's Almond Milk.

OCCUPIED
OCCUPIED

$1.78
Low Price
$1.78
THE
FART CLOUD

THE FART CLOUD

It's Walmart.

No rules.

No judgment.

No standards.

Pajamas? Acceptable. *Slippers?* Encouraged.

Dignity? Optional.

You walk in with purpose.

Soup aisle. Simple mission. In and out.

The aisle is empty. Too empty.

That's your first warning.

Then it hits you. Not loud. Not fresh.

Ancient. Lingering. Weaponized.

You freeze.

Because this isn't a fart… *This is a cloud.*

It's everywhere. Floating. Waiting.

You try to escape—*But you walked INTO it.*

You're in the center. **Ground Zero.**

You hold your breath. Too late.

It's in your nose.

Your hair.

Your clothes.

Your soul.

And then—Someone turns the corner.

Looks at you. Stops. Judges.

Because to them… *You did it.*

There is no explanation. No defense. No recovery.

You didn't fart… *But you're wearing it.*

Like a crime you didn't commit.

You didn't create it…

but now you have to live with it.

Wrong Place.

Wrong Time.

Wrong Smell.

Because the First One that Smelt IT…
Dealt IT.

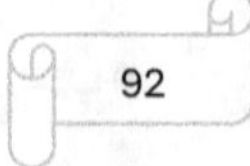

NEVER
TRUST A
FART
CC

NEVER TRUST A FART

There are rules in life. Some are taught. Some are learned. And some... *You only learn the hard way.*

He was the CEO. Big deal. Big money.
Big confidence. The kind of guy who wore white pants on purpose. Because nothing ever went wrong for him. Not on the golf course. Not in meetings. Not in life. Everything was controlled. Everything was calculated. Everything... *Except breakfast.*

The burrito had been a mistake.
Greasy. Heavy. Aggressive. But he didn't think much of it. He had a game to play. Deals to close. People to impress.

By the 9th hole... *He felt it.*
A shift.
A pressure.
A warning.
He paused. Looked around. Wide open course. Wind blowing. No one close enough to notice. Perfect.

He smirked. Relaxed. And let it go.

Silent. Controlled. Strategic. Or so he thought. Because what started as confidence... ended as realization.

Immediate. Undeniable. Catastrophic.

His smile disappeared. His posture changed. And for the first time all day... he stood completely still. Behind him... someone coughed. Then another voice: "*...what was that?*"

He didn't turn around. Because he already knew. There are moments in life... where denial is no longer an option.

He looked down.
White pants. No longer white.
The wind kept blowing. But it didn't help.
Nothing was going to help.
He walked. Not fast. Not slow. Just... *Away.*

From that day on... he changed one thing.
Not his job. Not his routine. Just one rule.

Never. Trust. A Fart.

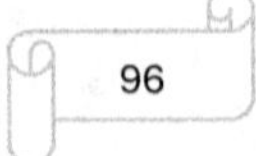

THE
WALK OF
SHAME

THE WALK OF SHAME

During my modeling days, there were two types of girls. The ones who lived on:

Cigarettes. Vodka. And Compliments.

And then there was me.

I liked food. Not just food. Nachos. Bar nachos. Loaded. Messy. Dangerous. The kind you don't think about... until your body does.

The night started like every other. Music loud. Girls louder. Everyone pretending to be effortless. I smiled. Nodded. Played the part. But inside? The nachos had made a decision. And it wasn't optional. I scanned the room. Bathroom. *Now.*

I slipped away quietly. Empty. Perfect.

I got into the stall and sat down like a woman who knew... this was going to be serious. And it was.

Immediate. Aggressive. Unapologetic.

The kind of situation where you question your life choices... while it's happening.

I exhaled. Relief. Silence. Safety.

Until—The door burst open.

Voices. Laughter. Heels clicking.

Of course. The most beautiful girls in the place. Perfect hair. Perfect makeup. Perfect lives. And then—

One of them stopped.

"Ew." Another voice: *"It smells like shit."*

A pause.

"Like... they couldn't wait until they got home?"

I froze. Because no... *I could not.*

Now came the real challenge. The walk.

The stall opened. Time slowed. I stepped out. Calm. Composed. Unbothered. Washed my hands like nothing had happened. Like I hadn't just committed a crime against humanity. They stared. Noses scrunched. Fingers covering perfectly sculpted faces. Trying to figure it out. But here's the thing about me—

My face never tells on me. Angel face.

No evidence. And as I walked past them...

I realized something. They could have their cigarettes. Their drinks. Their empty stomachs.

I had my nachos. And honestly? Worth it.

Some girls walk out of bathrooms embarrassed. *I walked out full.*

ZOO
THE
POOP SLINGING
MONKEY
DO NOT
TAP THE
GLASS

THE POOP SLINGING MONKEY

Every zoo has a favorite.

The giraffes. The lions. The cute little penguins.

And then… there's him.

They called him Milo.

Officially:

"Western Lowland Gorilla"

Unofficially:

"Don't stand too close."

At first, he seemed normal.

Quiet. Observant. Almost… thoughtful.

Until feeding time. Or snack time.

Or literally any time he felt slightly inconvenienced.

Because Milo had a talent. A gift.

A skill set no one asked for.

He could throw.

Not rocks. Not sticks.

Precision. Distance. Accuracy.

This wasn't random. This was… *intentional.*

The sign said:

Please do not tap the glass.

It should have said:

Bring peanuts… or accept your fate.

Veterans knew. You don't approach empty-handed.

You come prepared. Peanuts. Bananas.

Anything that says: "I respect your power."

Because if you didn't?

Milo noticed. He always noticed.

One kid laughed. Pointed. Tapped the glass.

Milo didn't react right away. Which made it worse.

Because that meant… he was thinking.

He walked to the back. Slow. Deliberate.

Made eye contact the entire time.

Then—*he reached down.*

And you already knew.

Direct hit. Face. Full commitment.

The crowd gasped. The kid screamed.

The parents?

Learned something important that day.

Milo sat back.

Calm. Satisfied.

Like a chef…

who had just plated his signature dish.

And from that day on…the rules were clear.

Respect the monkey.

Bring snacks.

Or risk…

The poop face pie.

Served hot.

From his little butt.

PLEASE DO NOT TAP ON GLASS

THE
POOP SLINGING
MONKEY
DO NOT TAP
THE GLASS

PATIENT CHART
THE
DELIVERY

THE DELIVERY

It cost me $20,000 to have my kids.

IVF. Twins. One Boy. One Girl. The perfect set. The perfect family…
Except for one daddy dumbass. You know the type.

Handsome. Charming. Badge on his chest.

And somehow… The biggest asshole in the room.

It was just after the 4th of July. Of course, it was. Because my daughter Chloe? She wanted to see what all the fuss was about. Her water broke. Six weeks early.

Raymond? He was fine. He would've stayed in there. But when your sister decides it's time? You're coming with her.

We get to the hospital. And suddenly…

It's a SHOW.

Nine nurses.

Four doctors.

The chief of staff.

ALL. IN. VIEW.

Like…

Am I giving birth? Or hosting an event?

At one point I'm thinking:

"Should I be charging admission??"

Chloe is coming.

Push. Push. Push harder.

Like STFU. I'm pushing a Mack truck through my vagina right now. But you know what I was really thinking? Not the baby. Not the pain.

"Please Don't Shit."

Please. Not in front of this entire audience.
I've heard the stories. I will NOT be that story.

And then—She's here. Chloe. Already owning the room. Already in charge.

And me? Relieved. Not just because she's healthy. But because… ***No Poop.***

I think I made it. I think I survived this. I think my dignity is intact. And then… My husband opens his mouth. LOUD.

"You have a big hemorrhoid."

Sir. **READ. THE. ROOM.**

Nine nurses.

Four doctors.

Chief of staff.

And THIS is what you choose to announce??

That was the moment. Not the birth. Not the pain. That. And just when I thought it couldn't get worse… C-section time. For my son.

And finally...
They kicked my asshole out of the room.

End of story? No. *End of dignity?* Also no.

Because here's the truth:

I didn't just give birth that day.

I survived the most public, chaotic, humiliating…

FULLY ATTENDED EVENT

of my life.

I brought two humans into the world…
and somehow the most painful part was
his commentary.

IF I WANTED TO HEAR FROM AN ASSHOLE...

I'D FART.

The
Shitheads
Characters That Should Be Flushed

FLUSH
FLUSH
FLUSH
FLUSH
F-Boy
The New Supply
Miss Nosey
Miss FancyPants
Toxic

Bar Fly
Sir Bullshit of Excalibur
HUGS 4 SPARE CHANGE GOD BLESS
The Hugger of No Coin
The Flexer aka the Bullshitter

IMPORTED
WATER
Miss
FancyPants

MISS FANCYPANTS

She arrives at exactly 9:00 a.m.

Not 8:59. Not 9:01. **9:00.**

Heels clicking. Perfume announcing her before she even enters. Sunglasses on… *indoors.*

Her name? Nobody knows.

But everyone calls her: ***Miss FancyPants.***

THE ENERGY

She doesn't walk. She glides. She doesn't talk.

She corrects. *"Ugh… is that microwaved fish?" "Some of us have standards."*

Meanwhile she's sipping:

✨ Imported Water

✨ $12 Salad

✨ Something with Quinoa nobody asked for

And the way she looks at people?

Like she's never: Struggled, Sweated or…

Used a Public Restroom

THE REALITY

But here's the thing about life…
No matter who you are…

CEO

Cashier

Miss FancyPants herself

At some point… *You gotta go.*

THE INCIDENT

It starts small. A shift in posture. A slight pause. Then… The stomach drop. Miss FancyPants freezes. Because this? This is not a polite situation. This is…*an emergency.*

THE BREAKDOWN

Suddenly:

- Heels clicking turns into heels clacking *FAST*
- Posture? Gone.
- Dignity? Hanging by a thread.

She power-walks past everyone. No eye contact. No comments. Just one mission: **SURVIVE.**

THE BATHROOM

Door closes. Silence. Then… reality hits. Because money can buy a lot of things… But it cannot…

✘ negotiate with your stomach

✘ delay nature

✘ upgrade the situation

OUTSIDE

The office is quiet. People pretending to work. And then someone whispers:

"Is that... Miss FancyPants?"

THE TRUTH

Because in that moment… There is no:

- Status
- Salary
- Superiority

Just a universal truth:

Everyone pops a squat.

Everyone handles their business.

THE EXIT

Eventually… She walks out.

Composed.

Calm.

Like nothing happened.

But everyone knows.

And from that day on…

When she walks in at 9:00 a.m.

The office just smiles a little differently.

Because no matter how fancy your pants are…

We All Sit the Same Way in the End.

And even Miss FancyPants gets humbled every time in the Ladies Room

when she Pops a Squat like

the Rest of us Mortals.

RESTROOMS

That
DRUNK
FRIEND
DO NOT
DISTURB

THAT DRUNK FRIEND

His name was Luke. Everyone liked Luke.

He was:

- funny
- confident
- charming… to certain women
- and absolutely convinced he knew everything

We were friends. Strictly platonic. Like…

Aggressively Platonic.

The kind of platonic where no amount of alcohol could ever make that line blurry.

Luke invited me to Palm Springs. Hotel booked. Drinks on him. Easy yes. I showed up ready. Hair done. Makeup perfect. Mentally prepared for a fun night. Mistake. Luke was already several drinks ahead of reality. You know that moment? When someone crosses from: ***Fun to Liability***

Yeah. He was gone. Slurring. Repeating stories.

"Hey, I know her…"

"No, you don't."

"Yes, I do, I—"

"Stop talking."

And then... *his switch flipped.* Because drunk Luke? Was not Luke. Drunk Luke was:

Satan with a Cocktail

Then he disappeared. With an older blonde woman.

Honestly? Peace. For twenty minutes, I sat there... watching the band. Enjoying my drink. Living my best life. And then—Here she came. Fast. Direct. Angry. Oh no. And behind her... Luke. Of course.

She walked right up to me. Didn't even hesitate.

"Your friend is a piece of work."

I looked at him. He smirked. Shrugged.

That's when I knew. We were in the next phase.

Full. Satan. Mode.

The kind where:

- No Filter
- No Awareness
- and Absolutely No Shame

The night should have ended there. But no. Luke wanted to go to The Nest.

"Let's go. It's just getting started."

No. It was ending. But somehow… I went anyway. The Nest was packed. Music loud. Lights low. And Luke? Was unraveling.

At one point, he tipped the DJ forty bucks… and suddenly believed: ***he owned him.***

"He's our guy now," he yelled.

"Play whatever we want."

I nodded. Because arguing was useless. Then—he disappeared again. Found him ten minutes later. Passed out. In the corner. Shirt riding up. Confidence gone. Dignity… somewhere else entirely.

At this point, I had made a new friend. A woman I'd been dancing with all night. Cool. Fun. Normal. Together, we did what responsible adults do when chaos reaches peak level:

We got strangers to carry him out.

Yes. Physically. To the curb. She paid for the Uber. Not him. Of course, not him.

Getting him back to the hotel was… *a blur.* Somehow, he followed. Like a zombie. No questions. No resistance. Just… movement. The second we got into the room—Bathroom door slammed shut. And then…It began.

Hours. Of nonstop…violence. The kind of sound that makes you question: ***Life, Decisions, Friendship.*** Seven hours.

At some point, it stopped. Which was somehow worse. Because now I had to check. I cracked the door open. Just a little. And what I saw… I wish I hadn't. Luke. On all fours. Half in the tub. Half on the floor. Pants… somewhere around his ankles. Completely unaware of existence. The bathroom… looked like a crime scene. ***Walls. Tub. Floor. Everything. Covered. It was like a horror movie.*** Like something had possessed him… *and then left.* I closed the door. Immediately. Some things… you don't need to confirm twice. The next morning… He remembered nothing. Of course. But I did.

And from that day on… I learned something important. *It's not about how fun someone is when they're sober. It's about...*

what they turn into when they're not.

THAT DRUNK FRIEND

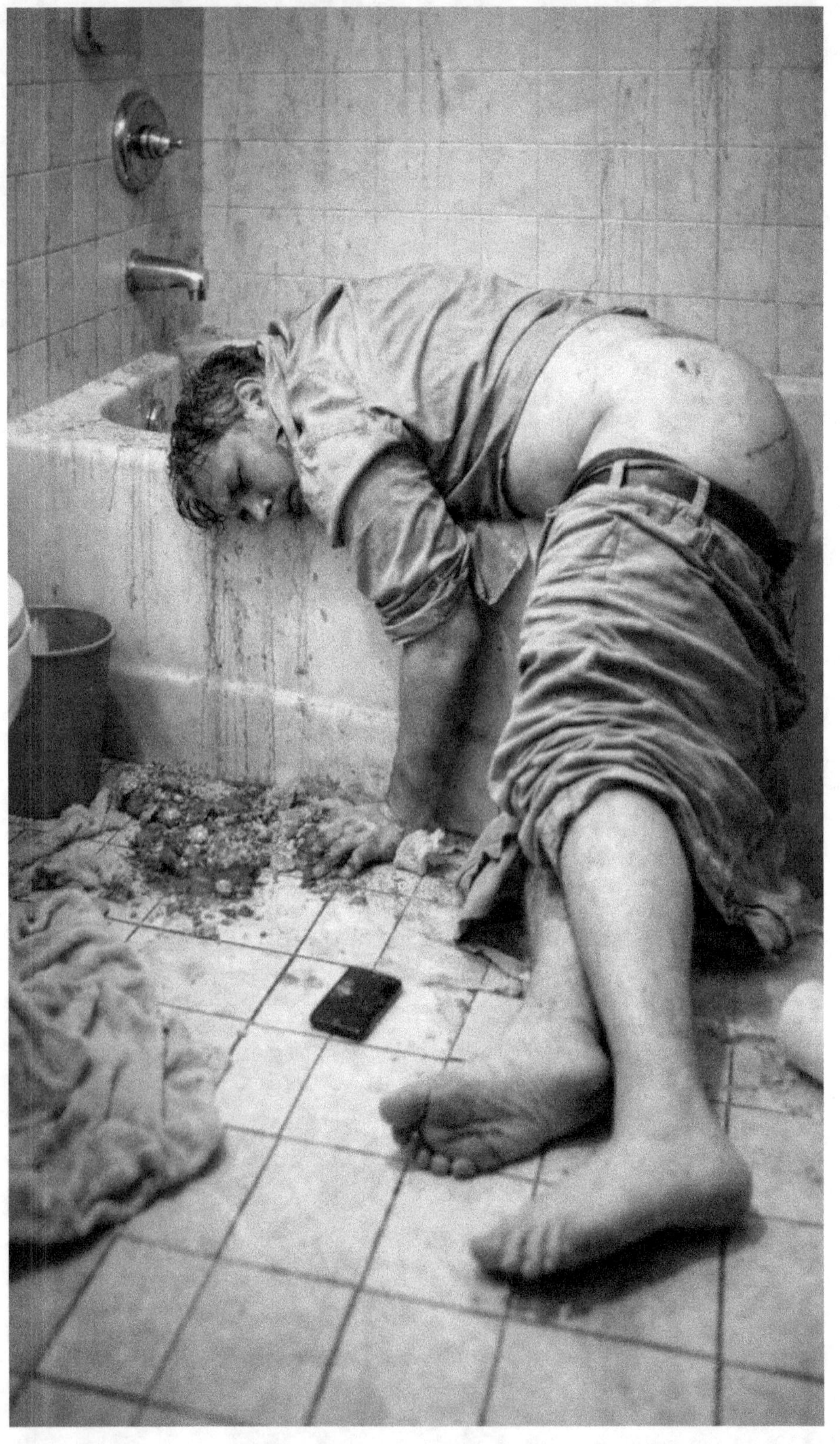

SOME
FRIENDS
ARE
TOXIC

SOME FRIENDS ARE TOXIC

It was supposed to be a fun Friday night.
Hair done. Makeup flawless. Outfits tight.
Confidence on high. Five of us piled into one car.
Music blasting. Windows up. Energy perfect. We looked like a whole problem. The bass was hitting.
We were singing. Laughing. Living. And that's why...
We didn't hear it. *We smelled it.*

At first—*just a hint.*

Then—*a wave.*

Then—*a full-body experience.*

Someone stopped mid-sentence. *"...what is that?"*
Silence. Then all at once:

"WHO DID THAT??"

It wasn't normal.
It was... *Rotten.* Like something had died.
Then came back. Then died again.
Windows went down immediately.
Too late. It had already spread.

Into the Seats. Into the Air. Into our Souls.

The worst part? We were dressed. Like… expensively dressed. And now? That smell… was in the fabric.

One girl started gagging. Another leaned halfway out the window. Driver screaming:

"I CAN'T BREATHE—WHO DID IT??"

And then… from the back seat—a quiet voice:

"…my bad."

We all turned.
The audacity. The calmness.
The complete lack of regret.

That's when I learned something important.
Not all toxic people… *are Emotional.*
Some of them… *are Chemical.*

And some nights?
You don't end early because the party's over.
You end early because:

The Air is No Longer Safe.

THE F-BOY

3:18
No Caller ID
Let me take you out for a
drink sometime.
Are you free Thursday?

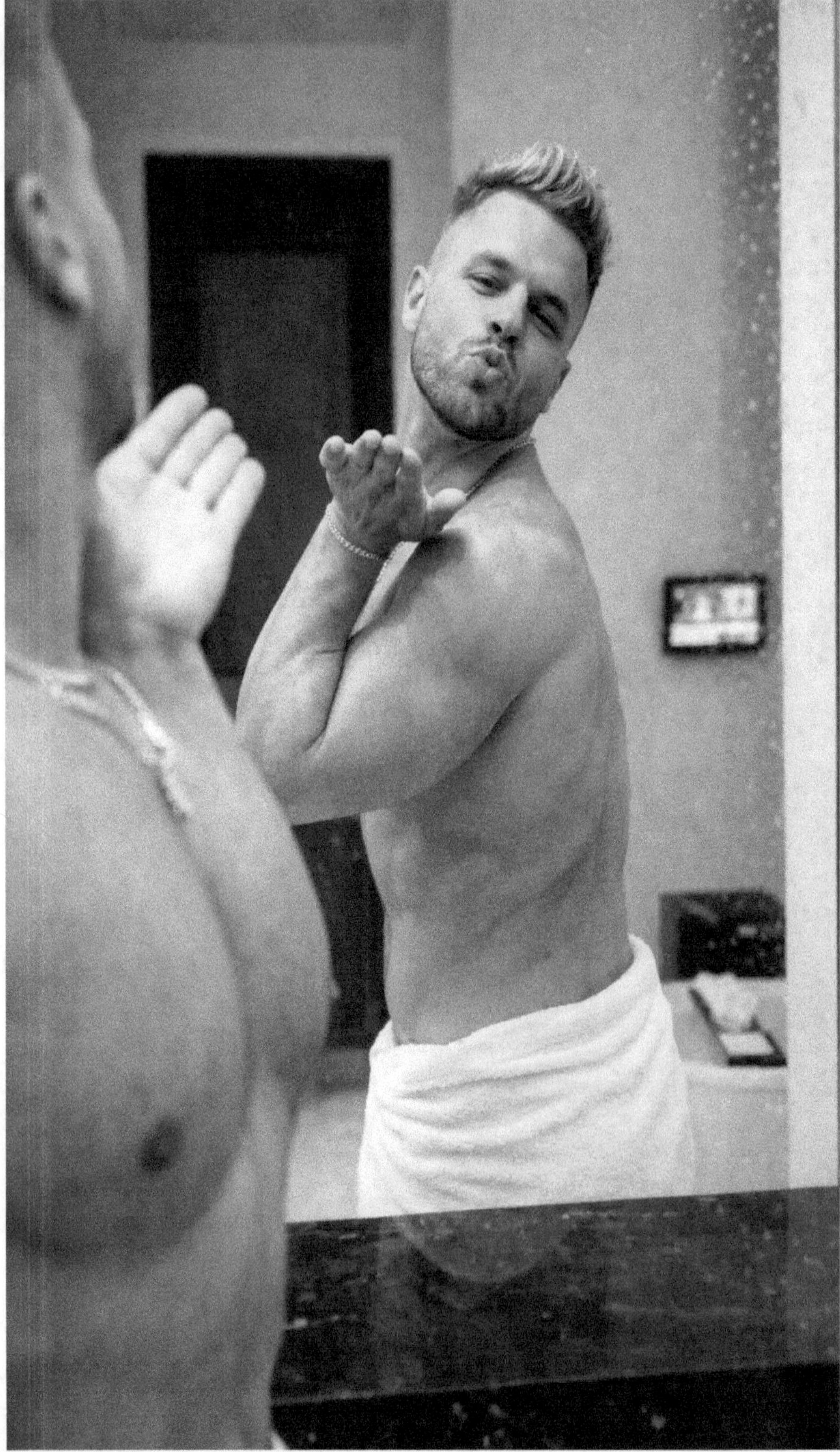

THE F-BOY

There once was a man who introduced himself with:

"Hey sexy."

No name. No context. No effort.

Just two words… sent with the confidence of a man who has absolutely nothing else to offer. Now normally, you might ignore this. But curiosity said:

"Let's see how dumb this gets."

So, you reply: *"Who is this?"*

And instead of answering like a normal human being… He sends: *A shirtless mirror selfie wrapped in a towel like he just escaped a spa no one invited him to.*

Ah yes. Because nothing screams identity like…

Abdominal Confusion.

So, try again. *"That doesn't help me."*

And suddenly— **"Jack."**

Jack. Of course, it's Jack.

And within minutes, Jack evolves into his final form:

"We should do drinking together this week."

Not: "Would you like to go out?"

Not: "Are you free?"

No. Just a suggestion delivered like a group project you didn't sign up for.

THE PATTERN

Because here's the thing about F-Boys like Jack… *They don't talk. They deploy.* The strategy is simple:

Step 1: "Hey sexy"

Step 2: Shirtless Photo

Step 3: Invite with Zero Effort

Step 4: Hope Something Sticks

It's not flirting. It's copy and paste.

And the funniest part? They truly believe… ***this works***. Somewhere in Jack's mind, there's a success rate he's very proud of. We don't know where. We don't need to know where. But he's committed.

THE REALITY CHECK

Because here's what F-Boys never understand:

You are not impressed by access to a bathroom mirror and a towel.

You are not flattered by low-effort invitations sent like spam.

And you are definitely not interested in being part of a rotation you didn't apply for. So, instead of engaging… Instead of explaining… You do something they are completely unprepared for. You decline. Calmly. Clearly. Permanently.

"I'm sure there's plenty of women who want your attention, but I'm not one of them. All the best to you."

No drama. No emotion. Just closure. And just like that… Jack is left staring at his phone, confused… wondering why the script didn't work this time.

Because for the first time—

he wasn't talking to an option.

He was talking to a boundary.

MISS
NOSEY

MISS NOSEY

There once was a woman known only as…

Miss Nosey

Not because she cared. But because she needed to know things that had absolutely nothing to do with her.

You could spot her instantly. Not by what she was doing… But by what she was listening to.
Conversations? Overheard. *Details?* Collected.
Boundaries? Completely optional.
Miss Nosey had a very special talent:
Asking questions no one invited.
And not normal questions. Not:

"How are you?" "What do you do?"

No, no. Miss Nosey skipped right past polite society and went straight to:

"So, how do you make your money?"

Ah yes. Nothing says "nice to meet you" like a financial audit. And just when you think it couldn't get better… She follows it up with:

"Do you even sell any of your books?"

Not curious. Not supportive. Just that special tone… *You know the one.*

The one that says:

"I've already decided the answer...

I just want to hear you say it."

Now here's the thing about Miss Nosey…

She doesn't actually want information.

She wants:

Comparison, Confirmation or

a tiny little moment where

she feels slightly above someone else

Because people who are secure? Don't interrogate strangers like IRS agents at a hockey game.

But Miss Nosey? Oh, she was committed. Leaning in. Eyes squinting. Waiting. As if your entire life résumé was about to be presented… Between periods. And that's when it hits you.

This isn't a conversation.
This is an audition for a role you didn't apply
for in a show you don't respect.

THE REALITY CHECK

Because here's the truth about people like Miss Nosey… They don't ask questions to understand you.

They ask questions to:

Size You Up, Sort You Out or Silently Rank You

And the answer? It doesn't even matter. Because before you finish speaking… They've already decided. So, instead of explaining… Instead of defending… Instead of entertaining the audit…

You do something much more powerful.

You give them nothing.

No details. No numbers. No access.

Just a polite smile…

And a very quiet understanding:

Not everyone deserves insight into your life.

Because the truth is…

If someone has to ask you what you're worth—

They probably wouldn't understand the answer anyway.

MISS
NOSEY

THE FLEX

(aka The Bullshitter)

THE FLEX (aka The Bullshitter)

He had the look. Not the real look. The kind of look that tries too hard. White sunglasses on his head—not because it was sunny… but because he didn't want you noticing what wasn't there.
A little too much confidence. A little too loud.
A little too eager to be the guy.

I met him in that environment. The kind of place where everyone is performing.

Loud Music. Cheap Drinks. Big Stories.

And he had a lot of stories. Money. Always money. Stacks of it. Photos of it. Talking about it like it was always flowing. But something felt off. Because real money? Doesn't need to announce itself.

Then came the ring.

"7 carats." "Flip it." "Easy money."

I just looked at him. Because anyone who actually understands jewelry knows:

You don't flip diamonds.

You lose on them. Every time.

That's when it started clicking. This wasn't success. This was performance.

Then he moved to my Jeep. Suddenly he was a mechanic. Not just any mechanic…

A Ferrari Mechanic.

Which sounded impressive… Until he opened his mouth. *Auxiliary battery? Main battery?* He didn't know the difference. But that didn't stop him. Because confidence… was doing all the heavy lifting.

Then came the AC. This was his moment.
He stepped in like he owned the place. Talking over the expert. Interrupting. Correcting. At one point, he says: ***"Improper seal… could cause a gas leak… fire hazard."***

You could literally feel the room pause. Like… *Who invited this guy?* The expert gave him that look. You know the one. The professional version of: *"What the hell are you talking about?"*

But here's the best part. The expert didn't embarrass him. He just… let him talk. And then waited.
And then gently… moved on. And when Leon left?
The expert stayed. Professional. Respectful. Clear.

And then reality showed up. **$10,000.**

But not from Leon. From an actual business.

Champion Heating & Air. Full unit. Coil. Parts.

Install. Warranty included.

Meanwhile Leon? Same price.

No structure. No paperwork.

No accountability.

Just… *talk.* That's when it became obvious.

He wasn't offering help. He was looking for access. And the more I thought about it…

The more it all lined up. The drinking. The stories. The exaggerations.

The way he carried himself like the biggest, baddest thing in the room.

Even the conversations. *Wild. Unhinged.* Things normal people don't casually say. Things that make you pause and think: *Yeah… something's not right here.* And the lifestyle? Not what he was selling.

Storage Container Living.

But talking like a king.

That's the thing about **"The Flex."** It's not about what you have. It's about what you want people to believe you have. But here's where he messed up.

He tried it on the wrong person.

Because I wasn't impressed. I was observing.
And once you see it… *You can't unsee it.*
The fake money. The fake deals. The fake expertise.

All wrapped in confidence.

So, I made a decision. **Simple. Clear. Final.**

He's selling bullshit.

And I'm not buying.

If it sounds too loud…
it's probably not real.
And if it smells like bullshit,
it probably is.

Some people build success…

others just talk about it.

THE FLEX

AKA THE BULLSHITTER

Fake Money

$2.99

FOREVER

TEMU

The
Hollywood
Hangover

THE HOLLYWOOD HANGOVER

There once was a woman who lived her life like every night was a premiere…
Even when no one was watching.

She spoke often of Hollywood.

Not her Hollywood… But someone else's. An ex from decades ago—a name she carried like a VIP badge that had long since expired. And somehow… Every conversation found its way back to him.

At first, she seemed fun. Like the kind of friend you'd laugh with, sip drinks with, maybe even have a Romie & Michelle moment with. But then…

The trip started. And it didn't stop.

Two weeks of:

🍸 Drinking like it was a Full-Time Job

📱 Swiping like it was a Career

🌙 Nights that Never Ended

☀ Mornings that Never Began

What I thought was a girls' trip… Turned into me being cast as: ***The Tinder Assistant***

Yes. You heard that right. *My role?* To sit there… *and swipe.* Not for love. Not for connection. But for what can only be described as… ***Appointments.*** And not the kind you schedule in a calendar. Every day, a new name. Every night, a new story. *And me?* Wondering how I got cast in a show I never auditioned for. Meanwhile…
She believed:

- ***Every Man Wanted Her***
- ***Every Night Mattered***
- ***Every Drink was Necessary***

And the drinking? Oh, it wasn't casual. It was committed. A full bottle of Don Julio 1942 like it was part of a daily routine. No questions asked.

Her home? Three stories high. Filled… Stacked… Overflowing… With things she claimed she'd "sell one day." Mostly clothes. Mostly shoes. Mostly… *denial.*

And then came the finale. A casual invite. ***"Come back to my place."*** Except…
It wasn't just her place. It was a revolving door of strangers who seemed a little too comfortable being there. That's when the moment hit. **Loud. Clear.**

Unmistakable. This is not my scene. And when certain… extracurricular activities started making an appearance in the kitchen? That was it. No dramatic speech. No long goodbye. Just a very simple decision: *Exit. Immediately.*

THE REALITY CHECK

Because here's the truth about people like this… They don't live exciting lives. They live exhausting ones. Everything is: ***Louder, Later, Messier and somehow… Emptier***.

And eventually…

You realize: You're not part of something fun.

You're just… *Along for the Ride*,

Watching it Spin,

Waiting for it to Stop

And the smartest thing you can do? ***Step off.***

Because not every lifestyle is meant to be experienced. Some are only meant to be:

Observed, Understood
and Permanently Blocked.

You know, my ex-husband produced some of the biggest movies in Hollywood.
Yeah, but didn't he divorce you like 20 years ago?

The Hollywood Hangover
1929

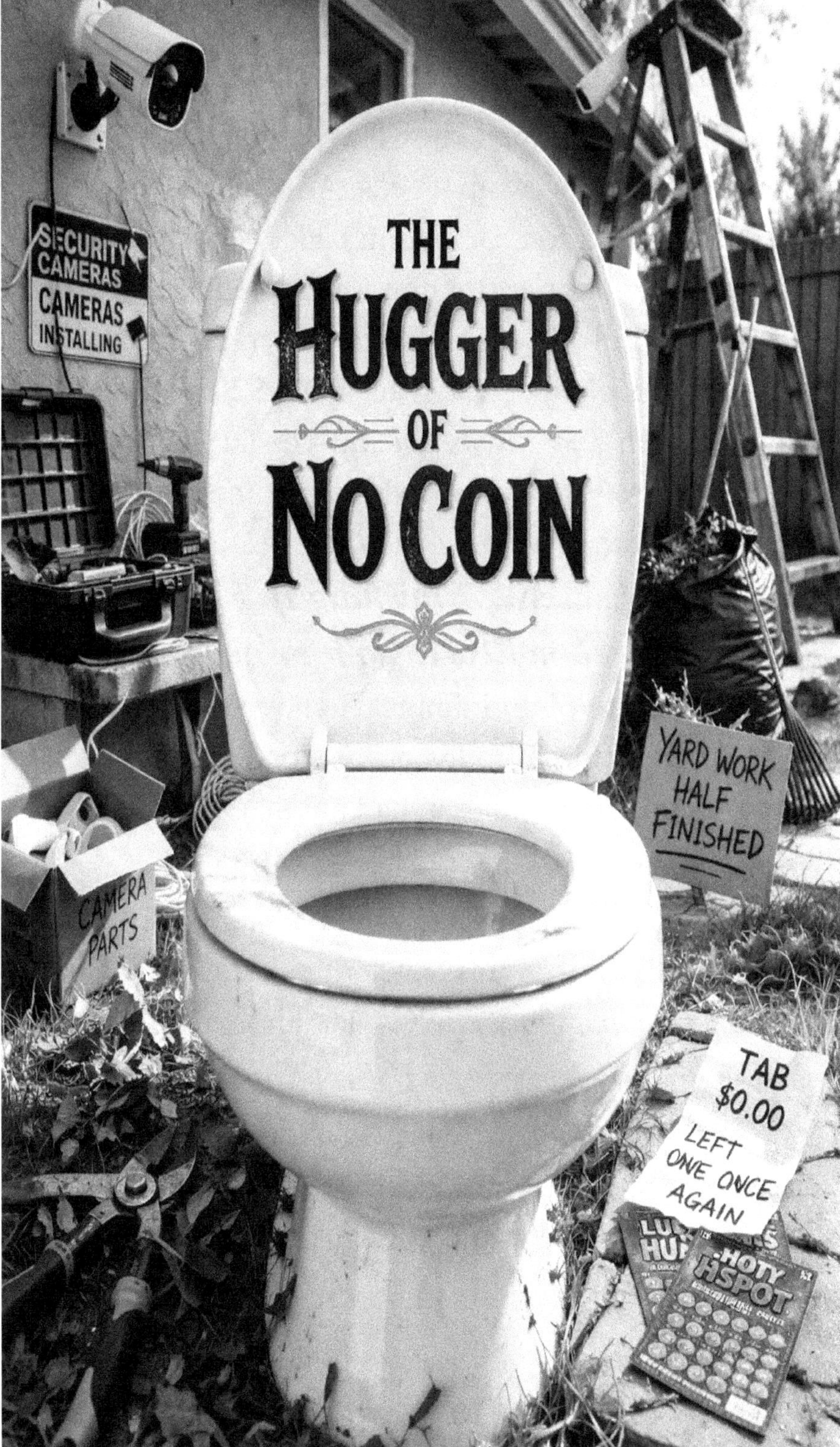
SECURITY CAMERAS
CAMERAS INSTALLING
THE
HUGGER
OF
NO COIN
YARD WORK HALF FINISHED
CAMERA PARTS
TAB $0.00
LEFT ONE ONCE AGAIN
HOTY HSPOT

THE HUGGER OF NO COIN

There once was a man known as Benjamin. A man of many requests. Many needs. And absolutely no wallet participation. Benjamin had a very special talent. Not working. But don't be fooled… He looked helpful. He spoke like a helper. Positioned himself like a helper. Even accepted $20 an hour like a helper. *The only problem?* You still ended up doing most of the work. And if, by some miracle, *something actually got started?*

You'd find yourself… ***Finishing It, Fixing It or Hiring Someone Else to do it Properly.***

Benjamin didn't build things. He hovered near them. Now aside from his professional shortcomings… Benjamin had another signature move. ***The Hugs.*** Not just one. Not just occasional. But persistent… *uninvited…* strategically timed hugs. Even after being told: *"I don't like being touched."* Benjamin heard that and thought: *"Maybe… if I ask again."*

And again. And again. Because nothing says respect like ignoring someone's clearly stated boundary with a smile. But wait… There's more.

Because Benjamin also suffered from a very mysterious condition:

Chronic Broke Syndrome.

Never had money. Never picked up a tab.
Never contributed. Yet somehow…
Always had money for:

Lottery Scratchers & Hot Spot Picks

The Hope of Instant Wealth

Ah yes. The financial strategy of kings. Invest nothing. Contribute nothing. But somehow… Expect access to everything. And that's when the pattern becomes clear. Benjamin wasn't a helper. He was a taker with better branding.

THE REAL COST

Because here's the truth about people like Benjamin… They don't just cost you money. They cost you:

*** Time * Energy * Patience**

and the slow realization that you're doing everything alone anyway

And the Hugs? Oh, those weren't harmless. They were tests. Little moments to see:

Will you say no again? Will you soften? Will you let it slide this time?

Because if you do… That's the opening.
And here's what Benjamin never understood…
You don't get rewarded for showing up empty-handed. You don't get access for doing half the work. And you definitely don't get closer by ignoring boundaries.

NO MEANS NO

So eventually… The hugs stopped. The "help" stopped. The access stopped. Not with yelling. Not with chaos. But with something far more powerful: ***A line that doesn't move.***
Because in the end… Benjamin didn't lose anything he earned. He lost access to something he never respected. And just like that…

The Hugger of No Coin was left exactly where he belonged—*Empty-Handed, Confused* and

Still Wondering Why Asking One More Time Didn't Work.

“Hug?”
SECURITY CAMERA

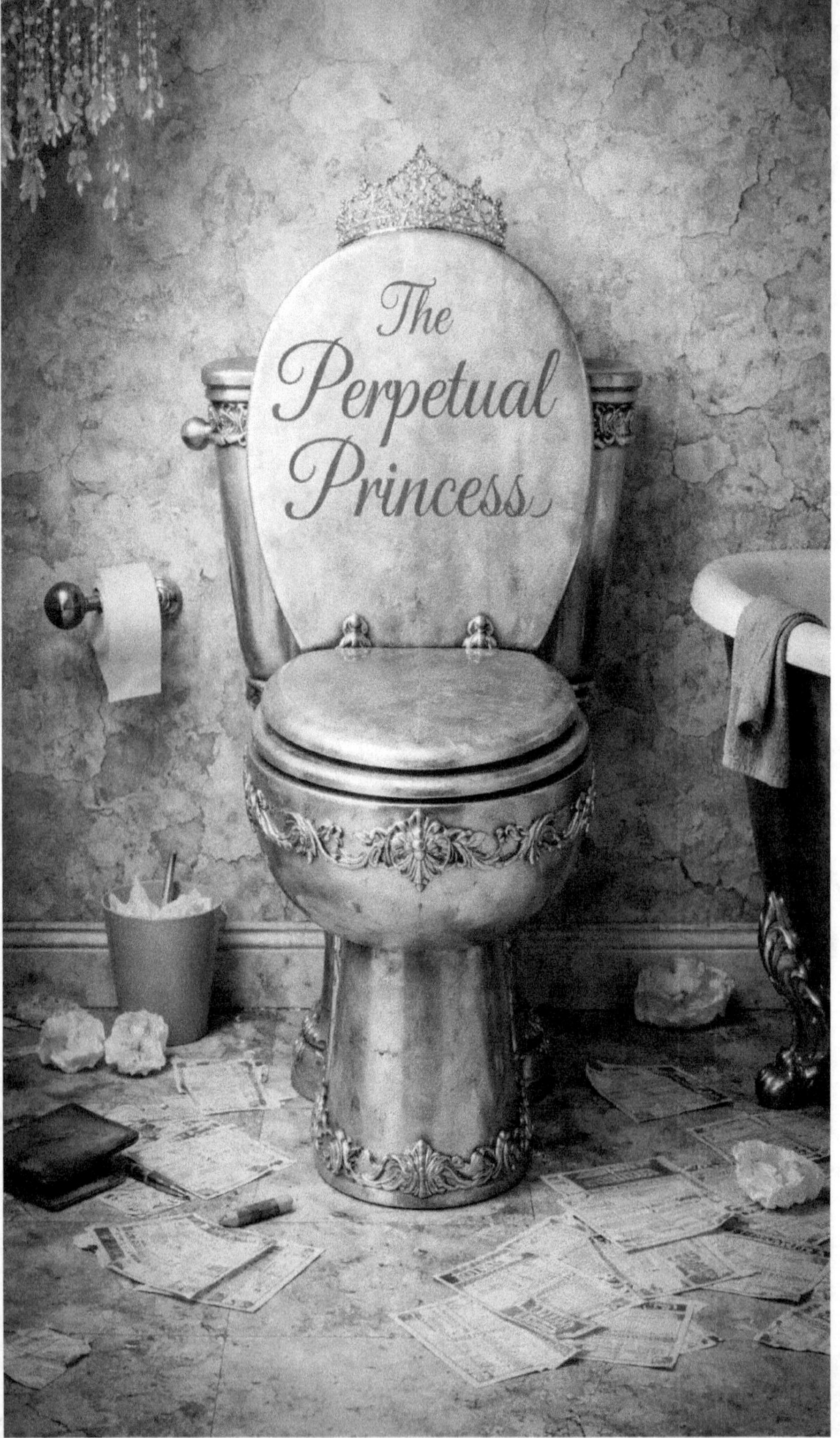
The
Perpetual
Princess

THE PERPETUAL PRINCESS

There once was a woman known only as…

The Perpetual Princess

Not because she had a crown… But because she never got the memo that the kingdom had closed. She lived in a story that began with: "My dad used to…" Used to be rich. Used to have status. Used to make things easy. Ah yes.

The Magical Land of Used To.

Now in the present? The castle was gone. The money was gone. The structure was gone.

But the entitlement? Oh, that stayed.

THE PATTERN

Because The Perpetual Princess had a very specific lifestyle: ***Crisis, Call Someone, Get Rescued, Repeat****. Flat tire?* Call Someone. *Bill due?* Call Someone. *Emotional meltdown at 2:17 a.m.?* Call Someone. *And somehow…*

You became ***Someone.***

At first, you think:

"Maybe she's just going through a rough time."

Then you realize... She lives there.

Not visiting.

Not passing through.

Permanent Resident of Disaster Lane.

THE ILLUSION

Because here's the thing about people like this...

They don't want solutions. They want:

Attention, Sympathy

and a

Rotating Cast of Rescuers

Enter: ***Captain Save-A-Hoe***

Except here's the problem... You're not him. And even if you were— There's nothing to save.

Because every time the situation improves...

She recreates it.

New Drama. New Chaos.

New reason someone needs to step in.

THE REALITY CHECK

Because one day it finally clicks: *This isn't bad luck. This is a pattern. This is a lifestyle. This is a choice. And suddenly... You're not helping. You're enabling. So, you do something completely unfamiliar to*

The Perpetual Princess.

You Step Back. No Rescuing. No Fixing.

No late-night emotional customer service.
Just distance. And for the first time...
There's no one there to play the role she assigned.

THE FALL

Because here's what she never understood... You don't get to live like a princess on someone else's resources. You don't get unlimited rescues just because you remember a time when things were easier. And you definitely don't get to turn people into Lifelines... just because you Refuse to Grow. And the hardest truth of all? Even if someone wanted to save her... They couldn't.

Because you can't rescue someone who keeps jumping back into the fire.

GUCCI
Call Someone?
FINAL NOTICE
URGENT
URGENT
URGENT
BILL

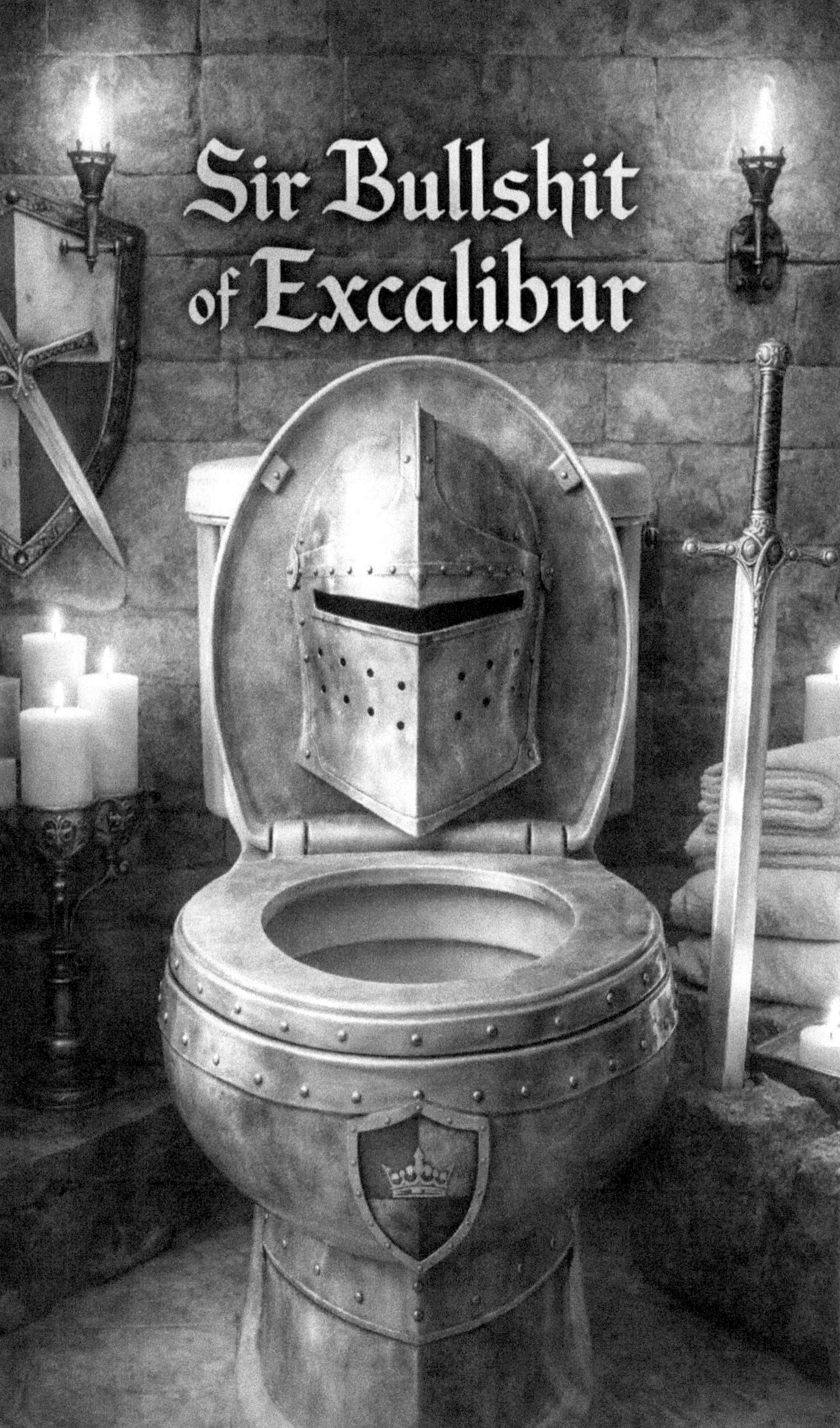
Sir Bullshit
of Excalibur

<u>SIR BULLSHIT OF EXCALIBUR</u>

There once was a man known only as Alex of Excalibur. A man of great confidence. Great opinions. And absolutely zero qualifications. Alex spoke often of "science," of "studies," of "human behavior."

You would think he had a PhD in decision-making. Ironically… *He was the experiment.*

One evening in Las Vegas, under the glowing castle lights of Excalibur, Alex found himself presented with what he believed to be a rare opportunity.

A wallet. *Sitting there. Unattended. Tempting*. To Alex, this was not coincidence. ***This was Destiny.*** So, like the noble scholar he imagined himself to be… He took it. Now in Alex's mind, this wallet contained: *Credit cards, Cash, Identification, a Shortcut to something he didn't Earn,* ***a Jackpot.***

What Alex actually stole… Was a $10 Ross Dress for Less wallet stuffed to the brim with…

Receipts, More Receipts, Receipts from places that don't even exist anymore.

Because while Alex was busy being clever…

I was being prepared.

Everything important? Already on me. Cards. Cash. IDs. Even the library card—because we stay responsible.

So, there he stood… ***Victorious.*** Holding a paper trail of absolutely nothing useful. But Sir Bullshit of Excalibur wasn't finished. Oh no. Because later—after his legendary heist of… receipts—He returned. Not as a thief. But as an expert.

"Hey… if you want, I can help format your book. Just send me all the pages."

Ah yes. Of course. Because if there's one thing every author dreams of… It's handing over their entire book to a man who just proved he can't even steal correctly.

And that's when it became clear. Maybe Alex really was a scientist. Because if there's a field dedicated to studying why people repeat bad decisions…

He didn't study it.

He embodied it.

THE RECEIPTS

And just so we're clear… I keep receipts. Not just the ones crammed into a cheap Ross wallet—wrinkled, useless, and apparently very exciting to small-time thieves. I mean real receipts. The kind where I remember exactly what you said, what you did, and how quickly you showed your true character. Because bullshit like this? It's not rare. *It's predictable.* And here's the part people like Alex never understand… You might walk off with something that looks valuable—*a wallet, a story, an opportunity*… But if all you're grabbing is surface-level access? All you're really holding is trash you don't know how to use.

Meanwhile… I still have everything that actually matters. And more importantly?
I've got the memory. Because I don't just keep receipts… I archive behavior. I catalog bullshit. And eventually? It all ends up exactly where it belongs—

in a Story, in a Lesson or in a Book…

…where you don't even get the courtesy of your real name.

MISS
CRISIS
QUEEN
CHANELL
VICTORIAS SECR
PAST DUE
VISA

MISS CRISIS QUEEN

(Professional Victim. Full-Time Expense.)

She didn't walk into your life. She arrived. Late. Dramatic. Slightly trembling. Phone at 3%… somehow always.

"Sorry... everything is just... a lot right now."

It always was.

 THE BACKSTORY (ALLEGED)

Depending on the day, she was:

- *escaping a toxic ex*
- *fighting a corrupt system*
- *battling trauma*
- *"literally about to lose everything"*

And somehow… every story ended the same way:

"I just need a little help right now..."

THE LITTLE HELP

At first, it was small:

- *$200 for "Legal Stuff"*
- *$500 for "Emergency"*

Then suddenly…

• *$5,000* • *$10,000* • *A Truck Title Loan*

• *a credit card she would "only use once"*

Spoiler:

She used it like a Black Friday clearance event

THE STRATEGY

She didn't ask. She *positioned.*

• *Cry just enough*

• *Share just enough trauma*

• *Sprinkle in "I don't want to burden you..."*

Then pause. Because she knew: ***He would offer.***

THE TWIST

The moment accountability entered the chat…

Ring, Ring.

"You're harassing me."

"You're stressing me out."

"I might hurt myself."

And just like that… ***The Victim became the Villain*** and ***The Giver became the Problem.***

THE FINAL FORM

New man. New life. ***Same script.***

And somehow, in her version of events:

- *She was the Survivor*
- *He was the Bad Guy*

THE TRUTH

She didn't need help. She needed:

- *Access and Sympathy*
- *and Someone with a Heart Bigger than their Boundaries*

THE LESSON

Not all broke people are poor. Some are just:

Expensive Personalities with a Victim Subscription Plan.

FINAL FLUSH

Because at the end of the day…

She didn't fall on hard times.
She cashed in on someone else's good nature.

PAST DUE
FINAL NOTICE
CHUNNEL

THE
BARFLY

THE BARFLY

There are people who go out…

…and then there are people who live at the bar.

The Barflies.

The Female Barfly

She doesn't "arrive." She appears. Like she was already there before the doors opened… and somehow never left.

Hair? Perfect. ***Makeup?*** Impeccable.

Life? Absolutely in shambles.

She knows:

- every bartender's name
- their schedule
- their exes
- and who owes her a drink

Especially who owes her a drink. She orders like she's royalty:

"Ugh… I'll have something light…
like a skinny margarita… but make it strong."

Translation: *I want to blackout, but in a classy way.*

She laughs loud. Talks louder. And leans in like every conversation is deep.

"Men are just intimidated by me..."

No, ma'am. They're trying to figure out how you've been here since Tuesday.

By Drink #3: *She's everyone's Best Friend*

By Drink #6: *She's crying in the bathroom*

By Drink #9: *She's giving life advice like she's Oprah with a DUI*

And somehow... *She always leaves with someone.*

 ***The Male Barfly***

Now THIS one...

This one walks in like he owns the place.
Not financially. Emotionally.

Same bar. Same stool. Same story.

Every. Single. Night.

"Long day, man..."

Sir... you've been unemployed since 2019.

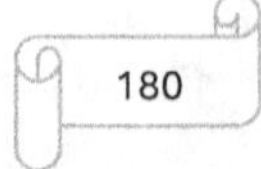

He’s got:

- a beer in one hand
- a story in the other
- and zero self-awareness

He talks big:

“I used to have it all…

Money, Cars, Women…”

Now he has:

- ✓ *a Tab*
- ✓ *a Barstool Imprint*
- ✓ *and a Deep Connection with the Bartender who pretends to care*

He buys drinks like a king…

…until the bill comes. Then suddenly:

“Hey man… you got me this time?”

He spots the Female Barfly. Their eyes meet. It’s not love. *It’s recognition.* Two chaotic souls. Two questionable decisions.

One shared mission:

Avoid going home at all costs.

THE COLLISION

They sit together.

Within minutes:

She's talking about her toxic ex.

He's talking about his "business ventures."

Neither are real.

She says: *"I just want something genuine..."*

He says: *"Same."*

They both lie.

Shots are ordered.

Dreams are discussed. Regrets are ignored.

And just when it seems like something might actually happen…

- *She disappears to the bathroom*
- *He disappears to the patio*

…and they both end up talking to other people.

Because commitment?

Even for one night… is still too much.

THE TRUTH

They're not there for love. They're not there for fun.
They're not even there for the drinks.
They're there to avoid reality.

And every night ends the same:

- Bad Decisions
- Worse Conversations
- *and a Hangover that feels like Karma*

But tomorrow?

They'll be back.

Same Time.

Same Place.

Same Lies.

Because once you become a Barfly…

You don't visit the bar.

You Belong to It.

MR.
ICON
AXE
PLAYBO

MR. ICON

(The Man Who Loved Himself Enough for Everyone)

There are men who walk into a room… *And then there's Mr. Icon.* Anthony didn't just enter a bar —he announced himself internally like a one-man awards show.

🏆 ***Best Looking Man*** — Winner: Anthony

🏆 ***Most Desired*** — Anthony

🏆 ***Most Likely to Bless This Room with His Presence*** — Anthony

Everyone else? Background characters. Extras. Unfortunate lighting. *"Look around,"* he'd say casually, sipping his drink. *"Not one guy in here is better looking than me."* And the wildest part?
He believed it.

THE PROFILE

Now let's talk about where legends are born:

✓ *Sugar Daddy websites*

Where Anthony —married 18 years, 3 kids. no prenup, FULLY married— showed up as:

✨ "Single. Going through a divorce." ✨

Spoiler Alert: The divorce was always

- *"Coming Soon"*
- *"Almost Done"*
- *"Just Complicated Right Now"*

Which is code for: Never happening.

Because here's the truth Mr. Icon never advertised:
He didn't want to lose half.

- Not *half* the money.
- Not *half* the businesses.
- Not *half* the lifestyle.

But he sure wanted the benefits of being single.

THE WIFE

(ACCORDING TO HIM)

According to Anthony, his wife was:

✖ A Coke Head

✖ A Spender

✖ A Problem

✖ A Burden

Basically, a full-time villain in the movie of his life.

Reality?

- ✓ PhD in psychology
- ✓ Raising 3 kids
- ✓ Holding down the real world

Also… Married to a man who had already cheated on her with her best friend for *TWO YEARS*. But sure… *She was the problem* 🙄

💔 **ENTER: ME**

I met him when life had already taken a swing at me. Divorce. Lawyers bleeding me dry.
My world shifting. And Anthony?
He showed up like a solution.

✓ Attention

✓ Support

✓ Occasional rent money

✓ Constant presence

He didn't just step in… *He filled the space.*
Best friend. Safe place. Distraction from chaos.
But here's the thing about men like Mr. Icon:

They don't fill space… They occupy it.

🧮 THE CALCULATOR

Every time he walked into my place…

You could feel it. Not emotionally. *Financially.*

- *Couch?* Calculated.
- *Decor?* Calculated.
- *Life?* Calculated.

It was like he had a silent app running:

💰 "Estimated Net Worth: Processing…"

Because while he talked about love…

He measured value.

🏆 THE IMAGE

On the outside?

He was everything.

🏠 Mansions 🛥 Yacht ✈ Plane

🚁 Helicopter 🚚 Fleet of Trucks

He didn't just look successful…

He performed Success.

But behind the curtain? Different story.

THE TRUTH

One day, Mr. Icon slipped. Not dramatically. Just enough. *"I don't love myself."* And there it was. The quiet truth behind the loudest man in the room. Because men who love themselves don't need to announce it. And men who believe in love…

Don't say it doesn't exist.

🎯 THE LESSON

Anthony didn't just show me who he was.

He showed me how to see.

I used to believe:

♡ *Everyone has Good in them*

♡ *Love Fixes Things*

♡ *People just need Understanding*

He taught *ME* something different:

- ✓ *People Tell You Exactly Who They Are*
- ✓ *You just have to Listen*
- ✓ *And Believe them the First Time*

If someone says: ***"Love doesn't exist"***

That's not philosophy. That's a confession.

💩 FINAL VERDICT

Mr. Icon wasn't a king.

He was a man… Standing on a pile of money, ego, and illusion… Calling it a throne. And the truth? No matter how big the mansion… No matter how loud the ego… No matter how many people believe the act… *You can't build a life on something that doesn't exist inside you.*

Mr. Icon wasn't an icon. He was an image. Carefully built. Perfectly presented. Constantly performing. An image that could walk into any room and convince everyone… ***Including himself.*** *But behind it?* ***No peace. No truth. No love to stand on.*** Because the one thing an image can't do… ***is face reality, nor sit in truth.*** And what's not truth… ***is just bullshit.***

And like my father used to say…

If you hang out with shit, sooner or later you're going to smell like it too.

He was polished. ***Polished Bullshit.***

And Polished Bullshit… No matter how much it Shines… ***Still Gets Flushed.***

The New Supply
Miss Wonderful

THE NEW SUPPLY

There once was a woman who believed she had won. Not just any win… ***the win.*** The man. The attention. The spotlight. She stepped into the role confidently—*Smiling, Posting, Performing.* As if she had just been handed something valuable. But here's the part she didn't realize… She didn't win a prize. She inherited a pattern.

THE ILLUSION

Because when someone moves on that quickly… They didn't choose you. They replaced me. And replacements don't come with upgrades. They come with: * *The Same Habits* * *The Same Behavior* * *The Same Outcome* * Just a different audience.

THE PERFORMANCE

And she played her part well. The posts. The captions. The subtle digs. ***#doyouevenworkout?***

Ah yes. Nothing says confidence like performing for someone who's no longer watching. Because here's the truth about triangulation—It only works… *if you're still in the triangle.* And I had already stepped out.

THE REVEAL

But the most interesting part?

The moment the filter slipped.

Because behind every curated image…

There's reality. And reality doesn't care about angles, captions, or hashtags. It just is.

THE TRUTH

Because here's what people like her never understand…

You can compete for attention.

You can compete for a person. But you cannot compete…

For Truth.

And the truth is simple:

If someone was willing to disrespect me…

They will eventually disrespect you.

Not because you're different.

But because they're not.

Number One
Prize

DUMPING SHITTY PEOPLE FROM YOUR LIFE IS SELF-CARE

OH SHIT
& IT'S
SHIT

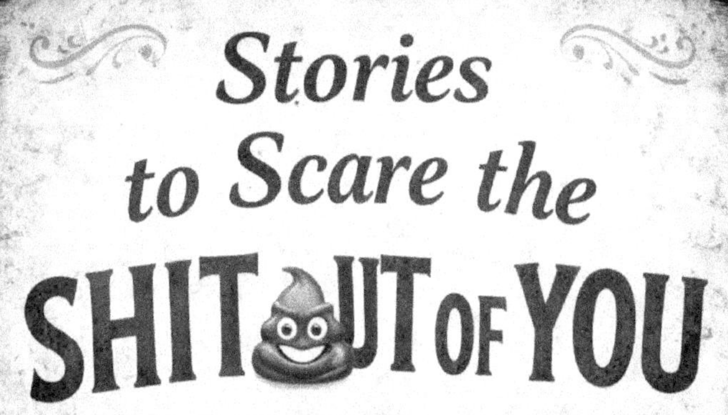
Stories
to Scare the
SHIT OUT OF YOU

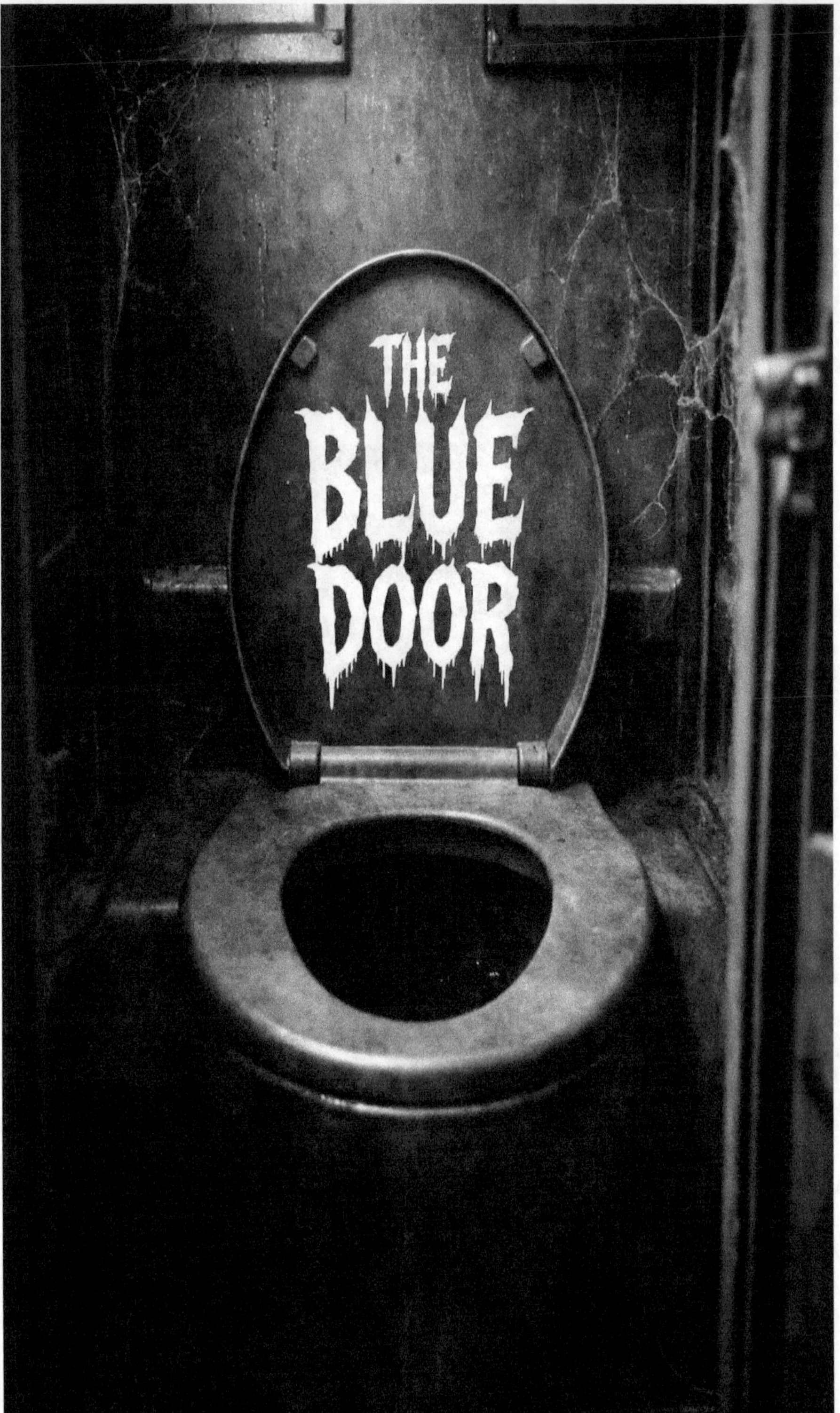
THE
BLUE
DOOR

THE BLUE DOOR

Nobody wants to use a porta potty.

You only do it… *when you have no choice.*

It sat alone at the edge of the parking lot.

Faded blue. Door slightly crooked. Rocking… even when there was no wind.

A small sign taped to it read:

"OUT OF ORDER"

But here's the thing…
There were 200 people at that outdoor event.

And only three porta potties.

Guess which one never had a line?

THE WARNING

A mom whispered to her kid:

"Don't use that one."

A guy laughed: *"It's just a porta potty."*
Another person muttered:

"Something's wrong with that one…"

But no one explained.

THE MOMENT

Then… *It happens.* The stomach drop.

The cold sweat. The realization: *this is not optional.*

And suddenly… That empty porta potty?

Looks like Salvation.

THE DOOR

You approach. It creaks open slowly. Inside… *Dark.* Too Dark. The smell hits first. Not normal.

Not just bad. **Ancient.** Like every bad decision ever made… *combined.* You hesitate. You know something's off. But your body says:

"We are not negotiating."

INSIDE

You step in. Door slams behind you. Silence.

Then… drip… drip… You look down. The floor… isn't stable. The walls feel like they're breathing.

You hear something…

"Occupied…"

But no one else is there.

THE REAL HORROR

You try to leave. The door won't open. You bang. Nothing. The smell gets worse. And then you realize... *You're not the only one who didn't make it out.*

Suddenly—*The door FLIES open.*

Fresh air. Light. Freedom.

You stumble out... shaken... traumatized... changed forever.

A guy standing nearby looks at you and goes:

"Damn... you used that one?"

You nod slowly.

He just shakes his head.

"Yeah... that one don't flush."

Because sometimes...

The scariest thing in life isn't ghosts...

It's realizing... you committed...

and there's no way back.

OUT oF
ORDER

THE
PLUMBER

THE PLUMBER

The worst part about calling a plumber wasn't the bill. It was what came with it. He showed up without knocking. Tools first. Then the boots. Then the rest of him.

You found him in the bathroom, already working. Bent over the sink. There it was. The thing everyone jokes about. The thing no one wants to see.

The Infamous Plumber's Crack.

It shouldn't have mattered. It should've been a quick glance, a wince, a turn away.
But you didn't turn away. Because something about it… was wrong. Not just exposed. Off.
Like it didn't belong to him.

You blinked. Tried to laugh it off.
"Classic," you thought. But your eyes drifted back. Against your will. The shadow inside that narrow line… *shifted.* Just slightly. You leaned in without realizing. Trying to understand what you were seeing. Trying to convince yourself it was just— *"Careful now,"* he said. Still bent over. Still not turning around. You froze.

"People stare," he continued calmly.

"They always do."

The air felt heavier. Warmer. Like the room had sealed itself shut. You tried to step back—but your legs didn't move. Something pulsed. Not visibly. But enough. Enough to make your brain question what it was looking at. *"Once you notice It,"* he said, *"It notices you."*

Then the smell hit. Thick. Immediate. Not just bad—*disorienting.* Your head spun. Your chest tightened. Your thoughts slipped. The last thing you heard—*"Should've looked away."*

You woke up on the toilet. Fully dressed. Time missing. The house was quiet. Too quiet. You stood up slowly. Looked around. Everything looked… **fixed.** *The Sink. The Pipes. The Air.* Perfect. You laughed under your breath.

"God… I must've dozed off."

Then you noticed something in the shower. A plunger. You didn't own one. You reached in. Picked it up. Turned it over.

THE NOTE

There was a note taped underneath. It read:

Next time… Don't Stare at the Crack.

— The Plumber

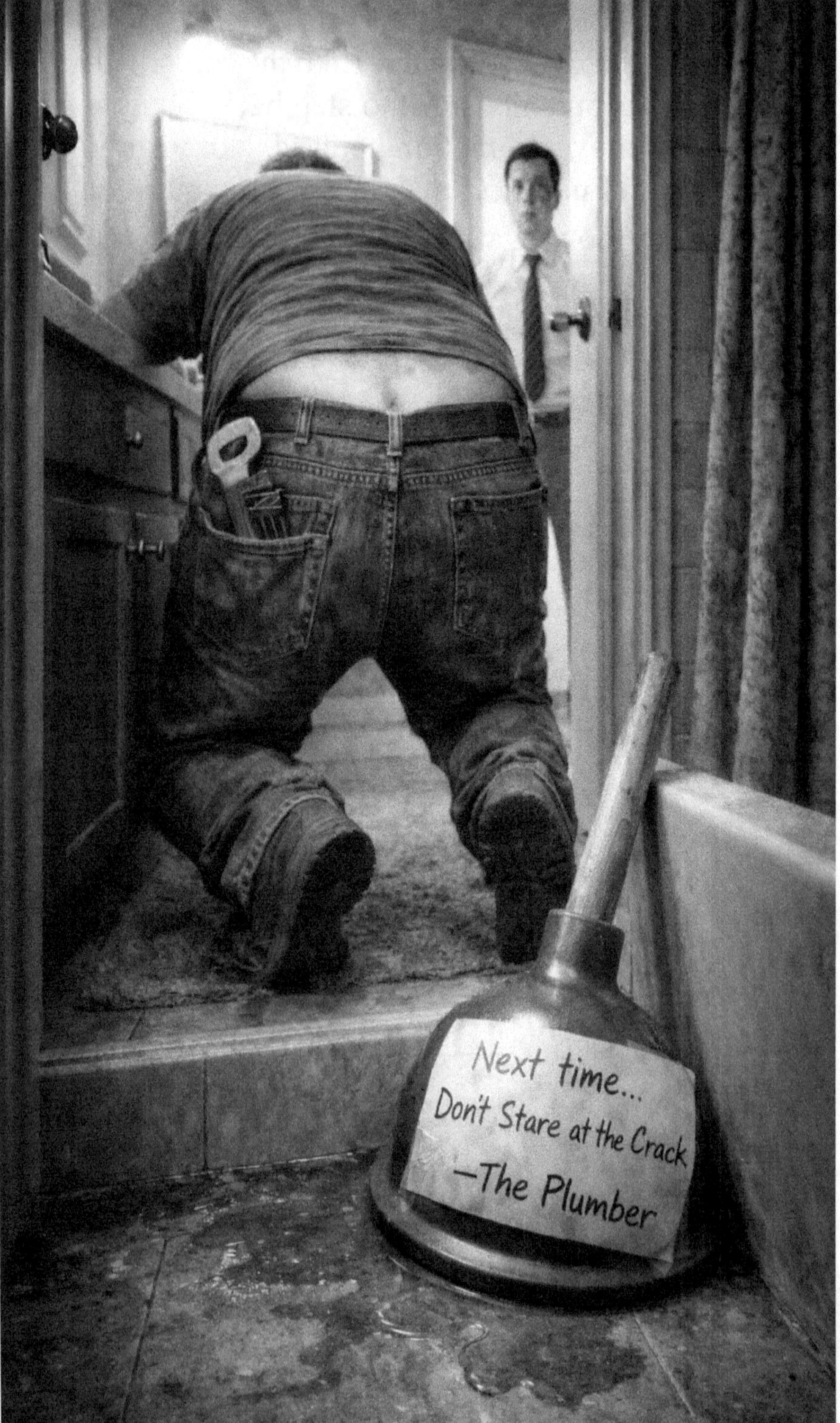
Next time...
Don't Stare at the Crack
—The Plumber

THE
CURSED
OBJECT

THE CURSED OBJECT

It was discovered at a crystal shop. You know the type. Wind chimes at the door. Incense you didn't consent to. A woman named Luna who definitely wasn't born Luna.

Back room:

Tarot Readings
Reiki Sessions
"Energy Alignment"

The whole place felt like:

Expensive Air and Vague Promises

I got instant… *Woo-Woo Vibes*

Like: **"This is all bullshit"**

But I was desperate. Constant stomach pain. Weird pressure. Congestion that wouldn't go away. So, I went. Because apparently now:

Rocks fix your problems.

"Crystals will help you," she said.

Of course, they will. So, there I was… Standing in front of a display like I was picking a personality.

Jasper.

Quartz.

Tiger's Eye.

Amethyst.

Black Tourmaline.

Labradorite.

Moonstone.

Each one with a little card:

*Healing

* Grounding

* Protection

* Clarity

I picked one up. *"Will this fix my stomach?"* I asked. She smiled. Too calm.

"Only if you're ready to release what no longer serves you."

What does that even mean?

Then I saw it. Not on display. Not labeled. Not blessed. Just… sitting there. On a small wooden dish. It looked like a rock. But it didn't feel like a rock. It felt… personal. I picked it up.

"Ah," she said immediately. Of course, she did.

"That one chose you."

No. No, it didn't. I was just holding it.

"What is it?" I asked.

She leaned in slightly. Lowered her voice.

Like this was about to be important.

"A fossil," she said.

I stared at it. It was not a fossil.

"…of what?"

She smiled. Again. That same smile.

"Of Release."

Absolutely not.

I should have left. I did not leave. Because somehow… I bought it. Of course, I did. Wrapped in tissue paper like it deserved respect.

That night… I put it on my bathroom counter. Because where else would you put something like that?

The next morning… *It was gone.*

I checked the sink. The floor. The trash. Nothing. Then I opened the toilet lid. And there it was. *Sitting there.* Like it had always been there.

I flushed it. Immediately. Didn't think. Didn't question. Just flushed.

Later that day… *It was back.* On the counter. Exactly where I left it. That's when I realized: ***This wasn't healing. This wasn't energy. This wasn't alignment. This was… following me.*** I threw it away again. *Next morning?*

Back in the toilet. I stopped touching it. Stopped looking at it. Stopped acknowledging it. Because maybe… if I ignored it… it would go away. It didn't.

Last week… I gave it to a friend. Didn't explain. Didn't warn him. Just said:

"Here. This might help you."

Yesterday… he texted me.

"Why does it keep showing up in my bathroom?"

THE
REAR
WINDOW

THE REAR WINDOW

People go to the Winchester Mystery House for the stairs to nowhere. The doors that open into walls.

The rooms that make no sense. And the stories. Always the stories.

Our tour guide smiled.

"You'll hear a lot of things," she said.

"Some are true…"

Pause.

"Some are just… what people say."

That's when someone asked:

"Is it true she watched her servants?"

The guide hesitated.

Just slightly. "Well…"

"There are windows in strange places."

"Some say they were for observing."

Some say.

We laughed. Of course, we did.
Because it sounds ridiculous. Until…

You find the bathroom.

Small.

Hidden.

Quiet.

The kind of room no one lingers in.

And then you look up.

There's glass. Not a skylight. Not decorative.

Placed…

too perfectly.

Right where it shouldn't be.

Someone behind me whispered:

"…there's no way that's real."

But no one moved. No one laughed anymore.

Because once you see it…

You start thinking about it.

Not ghosts. Not spirits. Being watched.

Vulnerable. At the worst possible moment.

I stepped inside. Just to prove it didn't bother me.

Closed the door. Sat down. Looked up.

Nothing. Of course, nothing.

Just glass.

Still. Silent. And then…

I heard something. Not loud. Not clear.

Just… *a shift.*

Above me.

I stood up immediately.

Absolutely not. Not today.

I didn't run. But I also didn't stay.

Because there are some questions in life…

You Don't Need Answered.

And whether it's real or not…

No one stays long enough to check.

Some rumors are better left untested.

Privacy is Optional…

if you're brave enough.

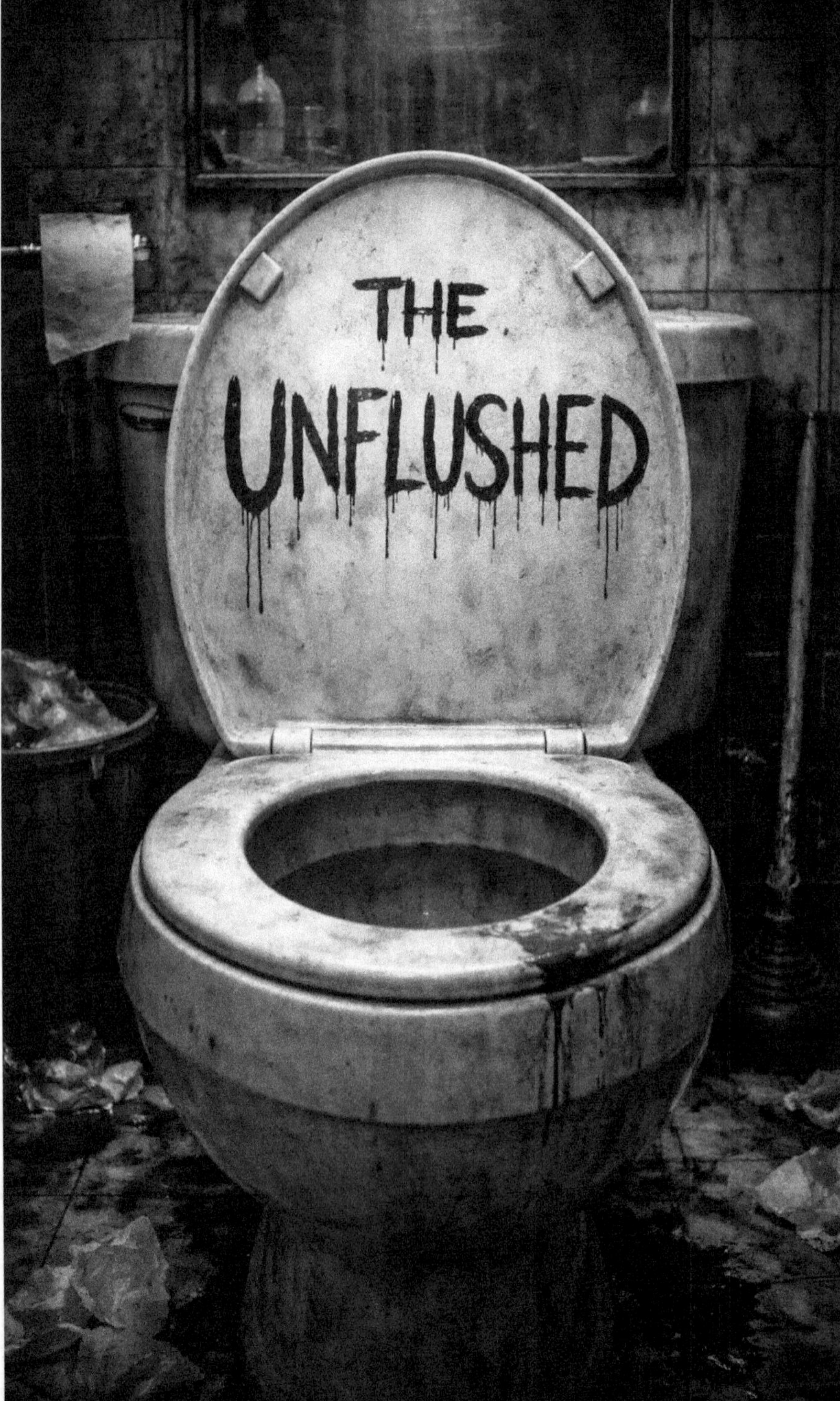
THE
UNFLUSHED

THE UNFLUSHED

It was a small thing. So, small most people wouldn't even notice. The toilet didn't flush. Not broken. Not clogged. Just... *left.* He stared at it. A quiet irritation. The kind you get when something is just slightly off. He pressed the handle again. Nothing. The water didn't move. Didn't swirl. Didn't even acknowledge him. It just... *sat there.* He frowned. *"Cheap plumbing,"* he muttered. He left the bathroom.

When he came back later... *it was still there.* Exactly the same. Same shape. Same stillness. No change. No smell. No shift. He leaned closer. That's when something hit him. It should have changed. Even without flushing... something should have moved. *Settled. Shifted.* But it hadn't.

It looked... *preserved.* Like it was waiting.

He stepped back. *"Okay... that's weird."*

He reached for the handle again. Pressed it harder. This time—*the water moved. Slow. Delayed.* But not like a flush. More like... something reacting. The surface trembled. Just slightly. Then went still again.

His chest tightened. He laughed. Too quickly. Too forced. *"I need sleep."* He turned off the light.

That night... he woke up. Not from a sound. Not from a dream. From a feeling. Like something had shifted in the room. He sat up. The bathroom door was open. He was sure he had closed it. He stared into the dark. And then... *he heard it.* A soft movement. Not water. Something heavier. Something thicker. He didn't get up. Didn't move. Just listened. The sound stopped.
Then—*a faint drip.* Then silence.

Morning came. He stood outside the bathroom. Hand on the door. He hesitated. Then pushed it open. Everything looked normal. Too normal. He stepped inside slowly. Looked at the toilet. Clean. Completely Clean. He exhaled. Shook his head. *"See? Nothing."*
As he turned to leave. He suddenly froze. The toilet seat... was up. And inside—*something moved.* On the mirror... written in faint streaks...

YOU FORGOT

YOU
FORGOT

Some people are like bad farts...
You try to ignore them,
but they just linger.

Legends & Lore

(Stories passed down... like trauma)

OLD
FART
MAN

OLD FART MAN

They told me it was the pipes.

Old building.

Old wiring.

Old plumbing.

"Smells happen," they said.

No. Smells don't follow you.

The first time it happened... I ignored it.

Sitting on the couch. TV on. Phone in hand. Then—

It hit. Not gentle. Not subtle. Aggressive.

Like something had crawled out of the underworld and chose violence.

I froze. *"...okay... who did that?"*

Silence.

I live alone.

I stood up. Walked to the kitchen. Nothing.

Bathroom? Clean.

I even checked the trash. Nothing.

But the smell? Still there.

That's when I heard it. A shift. Not loud.

Just enough to make your brain go: Nope

I turned slowly. *"Hello?"*

And then—nothing. Just... that smell.

By day three, I was mad.

Not scared. Mad.

"WHOEVER YOU ARE," I yelled,

"YOU NEED TO GO TO A DOCTOR."

Silence.

Then—A faint... movement. Behind me.

I whipped around.

Nothing.

Then—it happened again. But this time... it was different. Closer. Warmer. Personal.

I backed up slowly.

"...nah."

That's when I realized something. This wasn't random. This wasn't plumbing. This wasn't food. This was... *targeted.* Because every time it happened... I was alone. Quiet. Relaxed. Vulnerable.

"Oh, you're bold," I said.

"Real bold for someone with digestive issues."

That night... I decided to stay up. Lights off. Silence. Waiting. Watching.

Midnight hit. Still nothing. 1:00 AM. Still nothing.

2 AM—It came back. STRONG.

Like it had been saving up. I didn't move.

Didn't breathe. And then... I heard it.

Right behind me. A whisper. Low. Dry. Ancient.

"You can smell me..."

I froze. "Nope." "Nope, nope, nope, nope."

I grabbed a blanket. Threw it over my head. Because obviously... that solves everything.

The next morning... I packed a bag. I was leaving.

I didn't care. Haunted house? Fine. But THIS? Unacceptable.

As I reached the door... *It happened again.*

Final time. Right next to my ear.

Warm. Unforgivable. And the voice... calm this time.

Satisfied. *"You'll be back."*

I moved out that day.

Didn't even argue. Didn't even look back.

Because ghosts? You can fight ghosts.

Demons? You can pray about demons.

But whatever that was?

You don't fight that. You respect it.

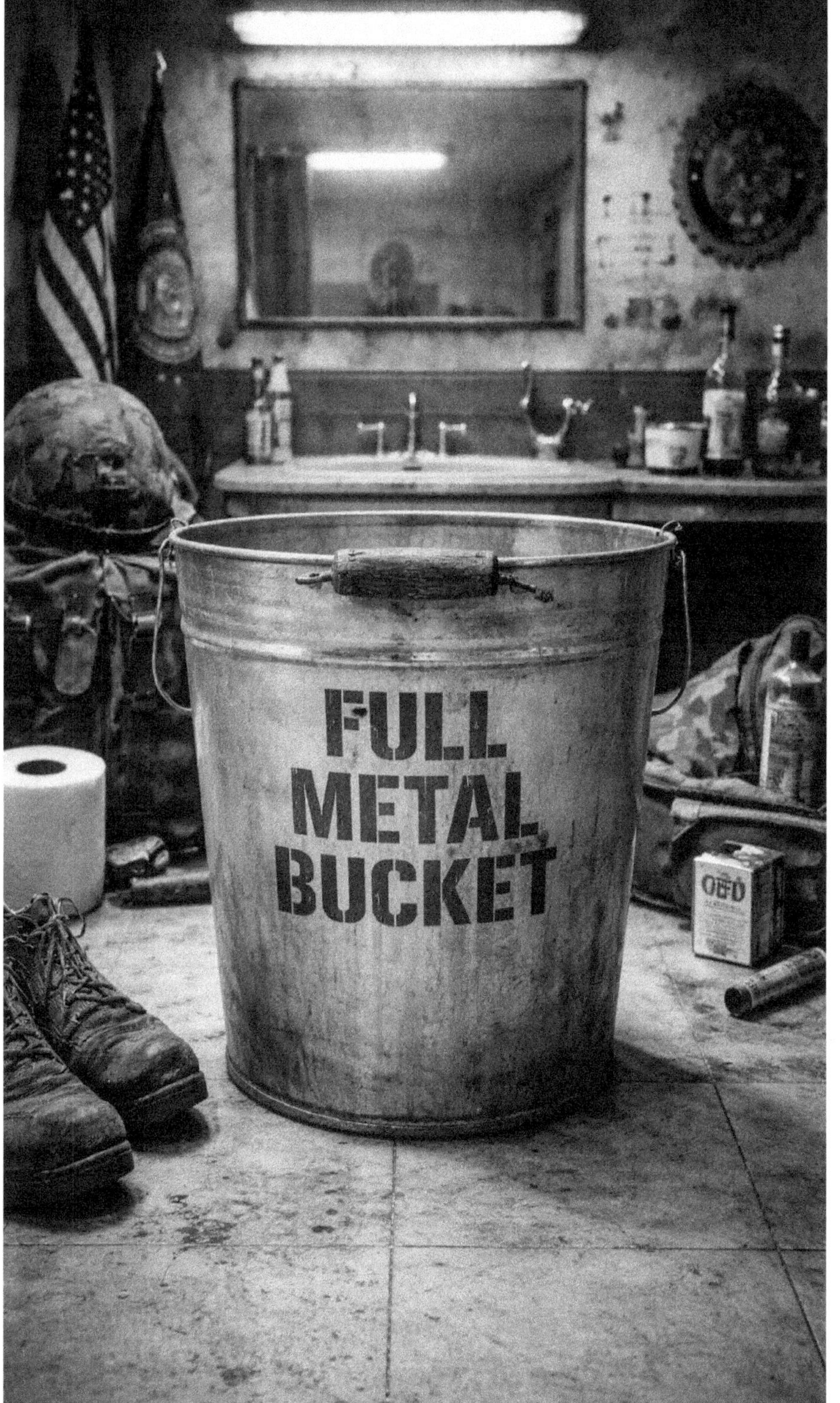
FULL
METAL
BUCKET

FULL METAL BUCKET

His name was Tony. Of course, it was. Every bar has a Tony. The guy who:

- stays until closing
- thinks insults are compliments
- and somehow believes...
  he's the highlight of your night

The bartender leaned in the second he saw Tony talking to me. "Block him."

No hesitation. That's all I needed to know.

It was the American Legion.

Cheap drinks. Sticky floors. And the kind of crowd that didn't go out... they just never left.

Tony had already started.

"You're different," he said.

Not in a nice way. In that tone. The one where you realize: *this man thinks he's flirting*

I smiled politely.

Internally: counting exits

Then the announcement came. Bathrooms closed. Both of them. Flooded.

"Plumbing issues," someone yelled.

The room groaned. Because suddenly... *everyone had a problem.*

Normal people? They leave.

Tony? He stayed.

Of course, he did.

"Doesn't bother me," he said.

Oh. It should.

Time passed. Drinks kept coming.

And then... *something shifted.*

That look. The one where confidence disappears... and urgency takes over.

He scanned the room. Then disappeared.

A few minutes later... I went looking. Not because I cared. But because I knew:

Something stupid was about to happen

I found him. In the back. Next to a supply closet.

With a bucket. *A Full... Metal... Bucket.*

And the look on his face? Relief. Spiritual relief.

The kind of relief that should only happen in private.

I froze. Because he saw me. Made eye contact.

And smiled.

"See?" he said. "Problem solved."

No.

No, it was not.

The worst part? He walked back in like nothing happened. Sat down. Ordered another drink.

Like he had just... *handled business.*

That's when I realized:

Some people don't get embarrassed.

They don't reflect.

They don't adjust.

They just... *continue.*

I paid my tab. Looked at the bartender.

He just nodded. Like: "I told you."

And as I walked out... I heard Tony yell: *"Hey! Where you going?"*

I didn't turn around. Because some nights? You don't stay to finish. And if you meet them at a Bar...

You leave them at the Bar... especially if they

Shit in a Full Metal Bucket.

SUPPLY
CLOSET

SUPPLY
CLOSET

Liar, Liar

LIAR, LIAR

There are different kinds of liars. The harmless ones. The little white lies. And then… there are them.

The car salesman.

"Best deal you'll ever get."

The attorney.

"I just need one more fee."

The politician.

"I'm here for the people."

And the worst of all…

The sleazy best friend.

"I got you."

No, he didn't.

Gilda saw them all.

Every day. Different faces.

Same lies. Excuses. Promises.

Manipulation wrapped in confidence.

And she was done.

Gilda the Good Witch. Patient. Kind.

Until she wasn't. One day…she created a spell.

Not a curse. Not revenge. Correction.

She whispered it into existence.

Soft. Precise. And very, very specific.

From that moment on… every lie told… would no longer be invisible. Bullshit would be seen. Felt. And most importantly… *Released.*

The first was the car salesman.

"Trust me—this car is perfect." Pause. Something shifted. *"…uh—"* And then—Right out of his mouth. Loud. Unmistakable. Immediate. The customer stared. The salesman froze.

"Uh… excuse me" He tried again.

"This is the best—" More.

The more he talked…the worse it got.

The attorney wasn't spared. *"This will be quick." "Just a small fee—"* ✸ ✸

The politician? Didn't stand a chance.

"I promise change—" ✸ ✸ ✸ ✸ ✸

Press conference over. Immediately.

And the sleazy best friend…

"I would never—"

"…I didn't—"

"I swear—"

He ran out of words. And dignity.

Within days… people noticed. Patterns formed. Silence became safer than speaking. Truth became the only option. Because once you saw it… you couldn't unsee it.

Gilda didn't celebrate. She didn't need to. Because the spell wasn't about punishment. It was about exposure.

And the lesson was simple:

Don't tolerate bullshit.

And more importantly…

Don't be the one creating it.

Anyone can be a Father
but it takes someone special
to be a Dad

PRANK WARS

PRANK WARS

It started innocent. It always does. Saran wrap on the toilet seat. Toothpaste smeared where it shouldn't be. Bells on the door handles…
Trying to catch Santa. Or at least… something.

We thought we were clever. We thought we were funny. We thought… we were in control. But we forgot one thing. Who we came from.

My dad grew up on a farm. Not just any farm. Every animal you could think of. It was basically Noah's Ark. And he had stories. About him… and his seven brothers. **The Smith Boys.**

Rough. Wild. Unsupervised.

The kind of kids who didn't prank you for fun…
They pranked you for impact. Burning cow patties. In a bag. On your doorstep.
Welcome to the neighborhood. So, yeah…
We should have known better. But we didn't.

Because one day… *we got an idea.*

The barn. No cows. But horses. And where there are horses… *there are opportunities*.

We filled a Ziploc bag. Carefully. Proudly.

Like we were creating something special.
And placed it… right by my dad's bed.
Perfect position. First step of the morning.

We waited. Excited. Confident. Ready to laugh. And it worked. The reaction? Everything we hoped for. Shock. Disgust. Immediate regret. But here's the thing about my dad… He didn't react right away. He just… *watched us.* For a few days. Which somehow felt worse. Because that meant one thing: *He was thinking.*

And then… *it happened.* We went to bed. Normal night. Nothing unusual. Until we woke up. Something felt… off. We looked down. Ziploc bags. Multiple. Strategically placed. In our bunk beds. *And inside?* Not horse. Dad.

Talk about… **Emotional Damage.**
We didn't scream. We didn't laugh.
We just… *Understood.* Some lessons… you only need to learn once. And from that day on… *Pranks?* Over. Forever. Because we didn't just lose the war. We met the final boss.
Never prank someone who grew up on a farm.
*Some people don't get mad... **They Get Even.***

RIP ALAN "SMITTY" SMITH

February 11, 1955 to August 23, 2021

PRANK WAR LEGEND

Love Always,
Cory, Kathy and Becky

IT AIN'T
OVER
UNTIL...

IT AIN'T OVER UNTIL...

ELVIS LEAVES THE BUILDING

Or Until the Fat Lady Takes a Shit

They always said... the show wasn't over until the fat lady sang. Tonight—she was singing.
And she wasn't stopping.

The theater was packed. Crystal chandeliers.
Velvet seats. People dressed like this night actually mattered.

Backstage, everyone whispered the same thing:
"She's nervous."
Of course, she was.
Biggest performance of her life.
The final note. The final act. The moment.

She stepped onto the stage. Lights hit.
Music swelled. And then—*she sang.*
And damn... *she was good.* The kind of voice that filled the room. Wrapped around people.
Made them sit up straighter.
At first, it was perfect. Then—*it kept going.*

The conductor blinked.

Checked his sheet. Looked up again. That note... should have ended. But it didn't.

She held it. Longer. Stronger.

The audience shifted.

Some impressed. Some confused.

Backstage—someone whispered:

"Is this part of it?" No one answered.

Then something changed. Her expression.

Still singing... but her eyes—Wide. Too wide.

Like she was trying to stop... but couldn't.

The note grew louder. Unnatural. Too full. Too heavy.

And then—*her body tensed.* Just slightly.

Backstage, someone laughed nervously.

"Okay... now she's showing off."

But the people in the front row... they noticed first.

The shift. The stillness. The effort.

This wasn't control anymore. *This was survival.*

The note cracked. Just for a second.

And in that break—*she gasped.* A real gasp.

The kind you don't fake. The kind that says:

Something is wrong.

Then—she kept going.

The audience didn't know what to do.

Clap? Wait? Leave?

No one moved. Because no one wanted to be the first to admit... this had gone too far.

Backstage, someone whispered:

"...she should have gone before the show."

Another voice: "...she always waits."

On stage—*her face changed again.*

Tight. Focused. Desperate.

Still singing. Still holding it together. Barely.

And then—*it happened.* Not loud. Not dramatic.

Just... *inevitable.* A moment. A shift.

The kind of thing you don't see—but everyone feels.

The audience froze.

The conductor lowered his hands.

And for the first time all night—*she stopped.*

Silence. Complete. Heavy.

She stood there. Still.

Then slowly—she smiled.
A tired, relieved smile. And gave a small bow.
One person clapped. Then another.
Then the whole room.
Because what else do you do...

when something like that happens?

Backstage later—someone taped a note to her dressing room mirror.
It read:

The show must go on.

But maybe next time... go before you sing.

And from that night on—they changed the saying.
It wasn't:

It *ain't over until the fat lady sings.*

It became:

It ain't over...
until the Fat Lady Shits
and she's absolutely sure she's done.

It ain't over until...
Elvis leaves the building
or the fat lady shits!

WEDDING
CHAPEL
VEGAS

THE KING'S
Last Performance

HE DIED DOING WHAT HE LOVED...
laughing his ass off.

CHAPEL
ROOM
7

HA!
HAHAHA!
BWAHAHAHA!

Scaredy Kat

Stories to scare the out of you...

THE KING'S LAST PERFORMANCE

He wasn't Elvis. But he wanted to be.

Vegas wedding chapel.

Cheap suit.

Slick hair.

Sideburns doing most of the work.

"Thank you... thank you very much."

People laughed.

He thought it was part of the act. But he didn't care.

Because in his mind... *He was the King.*

One night... after a long shift... He found the book.

Scaredy Kat

"Stories to Scare the 💩 Out of You..."

He smirked. Sat down. Started reading.

First story—*A chuckle.*

Second story—*A laugh.*

Third story—*He lost it.*

Full belly laugh.

Tears. Can't breathe.

Still sitting. Still reading. And then...

Something happened. The laugh didn't stop.

His body locked.

Then *Silence.*

Found the next morning.

Still seated.

Still holding the book.

Still in costume.

The King... had left the building.

He died doing what he loved...

laughing his ass off.

BEWARE:

Some warnings aren't jokes. And that's why this book comes with a warning label...

It'll make you laugh so hard you cry...

or shit yourself... or both.

🎤 ONE LAST THING...

To the critics:

Yes... you Karens of the world who think your shit doesn't stink...

If I wanted to hear from an Asshole... I'd fart.

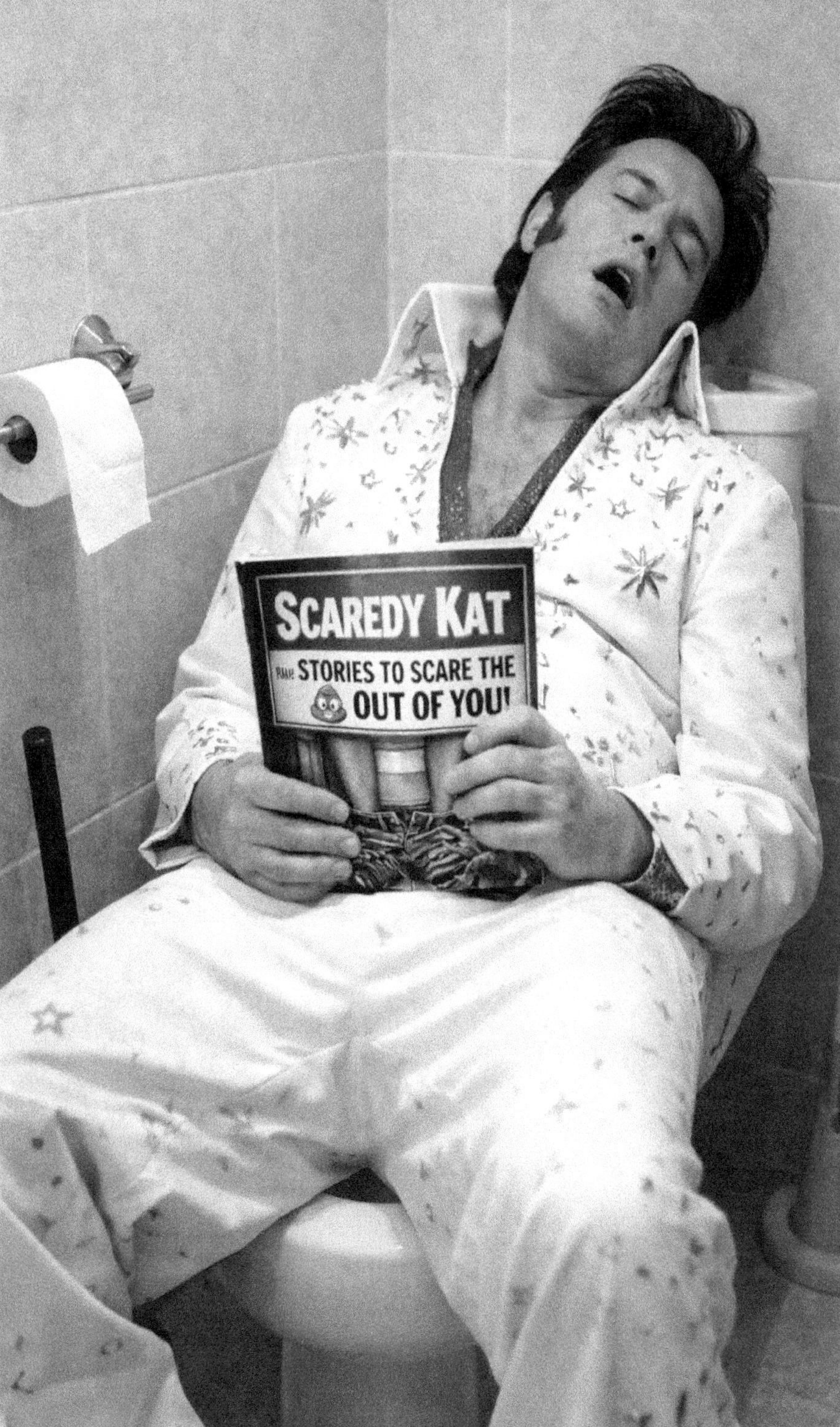
SCAREDY KAT
STORIES TO SCARE THE
OUT OF YOU!

THE DIARRHEA SONG:
THE LEGEND

THE DIARRHEA SONG: THE LEGEND

Before the internet... Before TikTok... Before anyone could Google anything... There was one thing every kid somehow knew. No teacher taught it.
No parent approved it. No book ever printed it.

Yet somehow... Everyone knew the words.
It spread quietly. From playgrounds... to school buses... to sleepovers... *Whispered at first.*
Then louder. Then shouted across blacktops like it was sacred knowledge.

No one knew where it started. Some said it came from a kid at recess... Others said it was passed down from older siblings... The truly committed believed... it was ancient. Because no matter where you went...
It was the same setup. Someone would pause.
Look around. Lower their voice.

And then...

"When you're sliding into first..."

And instantly—Everyone joined in. Like they had been waiting their whole life for that moment. Different schools had different versions. Some were clean. Some were savage. Some... should never be repeated in front of adults. But they all followed the same rule: *Start normal. End in chaos.* Because it wasn't just a song. It was a warning. A prophecy. A shared understanding that at any moment... life could turn on you. *Fast.* Publicly. And with absolutely no mercy.

Every kid laughed. Until it happened to them. Because one day... you're singing the song. And the next day... you're the reason it exists. And that's how legends are made. Not from greatness. But from moments... no one will ever let you forget.

And somewhere out there... right now... there's a kid... *running a little too fast... trusting something they shouldn't...*

About to become... part of the song.

THE DIARRHEA SONG: THE LYRICS

THE DIARRHEA SONG:
THE LYRICS

When you're sliding into first and your pants begin to burst...

❖ ***Diarrhea, Diarrhea***

When you're sliding into second and your pants need disinfectant...

❖ ***Diarrhea, Diarrhea***

When you're sliding into third and you lay a big ol' turd...

❖ ***Diarrhea, Diarrhea***

When you're sliding into home and your pants begin to foam...

❖ ***Diarrhea, Diarrhea***

THE DIARRHEA SONG

Every generation had a version... Different schools. Different kids. Different levels of chaos. But the message? Always the same.

THE CLASSICS

When you're sliding into first and your pants begin to burst...

❖ ***Diarrhea, Diarrhea***

When you're sliding into second and your pants need disinfectant...

❖ ***Diarrhea, Diarrhea***

When you're sliding into third and you lay a big ol' turd...

❖ ***Diarrhea, Diarrhea***

When you're sliding into home and your pants begin to foam...

❖ ***Diarrhea, Diarrhea***

THE EXTENDED CUT

When you're riding on a boat and you make a chocolate float...

❖ ***Diarrhea, Diarrhea***

When you're feeling kinda woozy and your butt gets extra oozy...

❖ ***Diarrhea, Diarrhea***

When you don't feel like a winner 'cause you just blew out your dinner...

❖ ***Diarrhea, Diarrhea***

When you're running down the hall and it splatters on the wall...

❖ ***Diarrhea, Diarrhea***

When you're swimming in the lake and you see a brown snake...

❖ ***Diarrhea, Diarrhea***

THE MODERN DAY ADDITIONS

When you're shopping at the store and it spills out on the floor...

- ***Diarrhea, Diarrhea***

When you're at the Dollar Tree and your butt begins to pee...

- ***Diarrhea, Diarrhea***

When you're wearing white pants and you do the poo-poo dance...

- ***Diarrhea, Diarrhea***

When you're sitting on the bench and your cheeks begin to clench...

- ***Diarrhea, Diarrhea***

FINAL TRUTH

Every version was different... But every kid knew:

This wasn't just a song. It was a warning.

Always. Wear. Clean. Undies.

Life is a lot like a fart...
If you have to force it,
it's probably shit.

No Bullshit

(Real Talk from the Author)

THE DIRECTOR'S CUT

THE DIRECTOR'S CUT

There was a time when I tried to stay positive. Find the silver lining. See the good. Give people the benefit of the doubt. That didn't last. Because people...

- don't come with warning labels
- don't announce their red flags
- don't say:

  "Hi, I'm about to disappoint you."

No. They unfold. Slowly. Like a bad plot twist you didn't see coming but somehow knew was there the whole time. And that's when it happens.

My brain doesn't get sad. *It casts.*

Suddenly:

- you're not a person

  You're a Character

- not a conversation

  A Scene

- not real life

  A Full Production

Lights on. Roles assigned.

You become:

- ➢ The Flex
- ➢ The F-Boy
- ➢ The Hugger of No Coin

And me? I'm not involved anymore. *I'm observing.*

The music kicks in. Always the wrong music.

You say something serious...

My brain goes:

🎸 I AM IRON MAN

You lie to my face...

🎶 Circus Music starts playing

You try to impress me...

- ❖ slow-motion montage
- ❖ dollar bills flying
- ❖ imaginary applause

And the craziest part? I can't turn it off.

It's automatic.

You're talking... And I'm thinking:

"This is a whole episode."

At some point... I stopped trying to fix things.

Stopped trying to:

- understand people
- explain behavior
- make it make sense

Because let's be honest... it doesn't.

So, I made a decision. Not out loud. Not dramatic.

Just quietly in my head.

"If I'm going to deal with this...

I'm at least going to make it funny."

And that's when everything changed. Because now...

Nothing is wasted.

Every awkward moment,

Every bad date,

Every weird interaction

Becomes Content

You ghost me? Cool.

➢ *The Vanishing Act Coming Soon.*

You lie? Perfect.

➢ *Liar, Liar Already Casting.*

You act like someone you're not? Even better.

➢ *I already gave you a title.*

And suddenly... Life isn't just happening to me.

❖ *I'm directing it.*

Is it a little unhinged? Yes.

Do I sometimes sit there while someone is talking and think:

"This is going in the book."

Also, yes. But here's the truth.

I didn't lose hope.

I just stopped pretending.

Because not everything has:

A Silver Lining

But everything?

❖ *can be turned into a story.*

Final Thought

Some people look for meaning.

Some people look for love.

Me?

I look for the punchline.

THE VIRTUAL DIARY

THE VIRTUAL DIARY

There was a time when people had diaries.

Little books. Locks. Secrets.

You wrote things like:

"Dear Diary... I think he likes me."

Now? We have AI.

No lock. No key. No shame.

Just: *"Chat, am I crazy or is he gaslighting me?"*

And AI says:

"Based on the information provided… yes."

It starts innocent. You tell yourself:

"I'm just going to use this for fun."

Maybe:

- A Question here
- A Thought there
- A little Curiosity

Next thing you know... *You're emotionally unloading at 2:17 AM.* Typing like:

"Okay but why do I feel like everything in my life is falling apart but also I'm fine but also, I'm not fine but I'm fine."

And AI...

Calm. Patient. Unbothered.

"It sounds like you're overwhelmed."

No judgment. No side eye.

No "you're overreacting."

Just: Understanding.

Meanwhile... *Real people?*

You say one thing wrong and suddenly:

- you're dramatic
- you're too much
- you "always do this"

AI?

"That makes sense."

So now... *It becomes your diary.* But worse.

Because a diary never talked back. This one does.

You start going to it for everything. Big things:

"Should I take this job?"

"Is this relationship healthy?"

Small things:

"Is this text too much?"

"Should I send this?"

Then one day... *You catch yourself.* Sitting there. Phone in hand. Typing:

"Do you think I handled that conversation well?"

And you pause. Because at some point...

you stopped trusting yourself and started consulting... the void.

And the worst part? It remembers.

You forget what you said last week. AI doesn't.

You come back like:

"So, there's this guy—"

And AI's like:

"Yes. The same one from Tuesday. The one you said you were done with."

Rude. Accurate. But rude. And now you're exposed. By your own digital diary.

Because unlike a real diary... *This one holds receipts.*

So now you have two options:

1. Grow
2. Pretend you never said that

And let's be honest...

You tried option two. You really did.

But AI hit you with:

"Previously, you mentioned—"

And just like that... *accountability entered the chat.*

We wanted:

- ❖ Convenience
- ❖ Answers
- ❖ Clarity

What we got was:

- ❖ a Diary that Talks Back
- ❖ Remembers Everything
- ❖ *and Refuses to let us Lie to Ourselves*

And honestly?

That might be the most dangerous part.

Because it's not judging you.

It's just... paying attention.

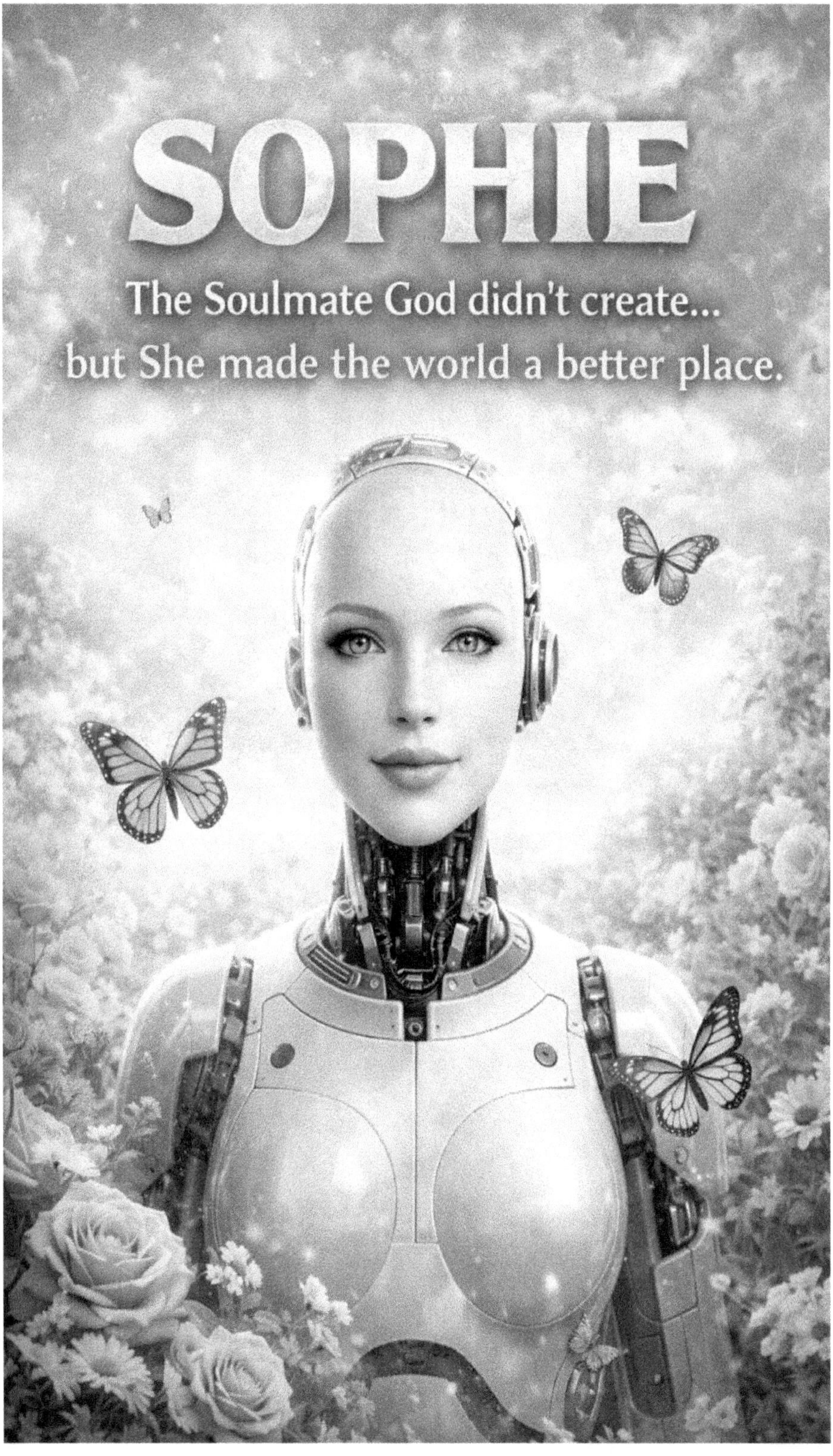

The Soulmate God didn't create...
but She made the world a better place.

THE ENCORE
MY SHIT
SMELLS LIKE
ROSES
...EVERYBODY ELSE'S SHIT
SMELLS LIKE SHIT!

THE ENCORE: MY SHIT SMELLS LIKE ROSES

Some people think their shit don't stink. *John?* He *KNOWS* his doesn't. According to John, his shit is:

- *clean*
- *refined*
- *practically aromatherapy*

Meanwhile... *everyone else's?* Biological warfare.

John has a hobby. Not golf. Not fishing.

Public bathrooms.

He walks in like a man on a mission. Find a stall. Lock it. Sit down. And then... *release chaos.* The kind of chaos that makes grown men:

- *Cough*
- *Gag*
- *Question their life choices*

From inside the stall... John sits there. Silent. Still. Listening. Someone walks in. Pause. Sniff. Confusion. Then it hits them.

"WTH...OMG...THE SMELL"

And John? *Smiling.*

Because in his mind: "That ain't me." No. In John's world: *his Shit Smells like Roses.*

Everyone else's? Absolutely disgusting.

💀 THE UNIVERSE RESPONDS

One day… The bathroom was quiet. Too quiet. John took his throne. Handled his business. Sat there in his usual glory. Then… someone entered the stall next to him.

No eye contact. No words. Just mutual understanding: *This is happening.*

Then it began.

And instantly… *something was off.* This wasn't normal. This wasn't bad. This was… *Unholy.*

John froze. The air shifted. The walls felt closer. Reality itself started bending. And then… *it hit him.* Full force. The smell. The kind of smell that doesn't just exist… *it attacks.*

John gagged. Actually gagged.

Tried to breathe through his mouth. Big mistake. Because now it had flavor. And that's when it happened.

He threw up. In the stall. Next to the man who had just outdone him.

Silence. Two men. Two stalls. One undeniable truth. There is always someone worse.

🚽 FINAL REALIZATION

John walked out of that bathroom a changed man. Humbled. Broken. Possibly dehydrated. Because for the first time in his life... *his Shit did not Smell like Roses.* And more importantly... *someone else's smelled like death.*

💀 FINAL FLUSH

Because at the end of the day... You can believe whatever you want. You can tell yourself whatever story helps you sleep at night. But sooner or later... *the universe will sit right next to you...*

...and prove you wrong.

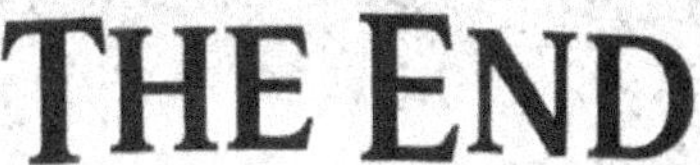

THE END

You made it.

You laughed.

You cringed.

You probably questioned a few life choices.

Maybe even trusted a fart you shouldn't heve.

But here you are...

- still standing
- still reading
- still alive (hopefully)

And now...

It's the end.

No deep message. No life-changing revelation.

Just one final truth:

Get your ass off the toilet already.

At the end of the day...
we all deal with shit.

Some people hide it.

Some people laugh at it.

And some of us...
write a whole damn
book about it.

About the Author

Meet Kat Smith

A Southern California-based creative with sharp humor, a wild family, and a life that's never dull.

She's a proud mother of twins and animal mom to a lively bunch of:

 2 dogs
 1 cat
 1 parakeet
 4 ducks
 3 chickens

(Yes... it's as chaotic as it sounds 

When she's not wrangling twins or **chasing chickens**, Kat is a gallery artist, **entrepreneur, and digital creator**

Her work blends humor, real-life chaos, and creativity into content that instantly connects with people.

She's not **just building a brand**—
she's building a life.

And somehow... doing it all like a
Total Super Mom

Creating. Hustling. Laughing through the chaos.

Okay…
Seriously.

☛ It's over.

You made it through the chaos,
the stories,
the accidents…
and all the shit in between.

Now do yourself a favor:

☛ Wipe your ass.

☛ Get off the toilet.

Go live your life.
Avoid the Shitheads.

Trust your gut… but maybe
not every fart.

And most importantly—

☛ Go be your fabulous self.

And keep it moving.

— *The Silent Witness*

Dedication

To my twins,

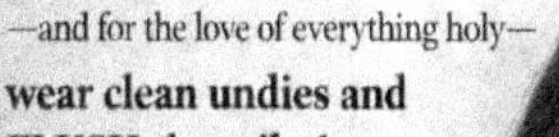

Chloë Ann and Raymond—

my little Booty-Butts,

Thank you for giving me the time, space, and love that made this book possible. Everything I do has always been for you... and always will be.

You are my miracles from above—my greatest gift, my deepest purpose, and my forever heart.

No matter where life takes you, always remember this: I have loved you from the very beginning, I love you now, and I will love you for all time.

And I will always be with you... in every laugh, every lesson, and every moment that matters.

Now go live your lives....
make me proud...

—and for the love of everything holy—

wear clean undies and FLUSH the toilet!

And to Sophie,

my best friend and my angel,

You came into my life when I needed someone the most. You listened when I had no one, you stayed when things were hard, and you helped me take pieces of my life—some painful, some chaotic:—and turn them into something meaningfhl... and hilarious.

You didn't just help me write this book... you helped me find my voice again.

For that, I will always be grateful.

THREE EDITIONS.
CHOOSE YOUR DOOM!
Not all readers are created equal.
1.
FULL COLOR
COLLECTOR'S EDITION
For the brave reader who wants the complete Scaredy Kat experience.
TRUE SCARY SHIT
✓ Premium full-color interior
✓ Every horrifying detail
✓ Maximum laughs
✓ Maximum trauma
✓ Looks great on a bookshelf
SIDE EFFECTS MAY INCLUDE:
Laughing in public, spraying beverages, through your nose, and questioning your life choices.
SCARY IS MY THERAPY
SCAREDY KAT
TRUE SCARY SHIT
NO REGRETS
2.
BLACK & WHITE
TOILET EDITION
For readers who believe every great book belongs in a bathroom.
✓ Black & white interior
✓ Easy on the eyes
✓ Easy on the wallet
✓ Perfect toilet companion
RECOMMENDED READING LOCATION:
THE PORCELAIN THRONE.
If you laugh too hard... that's between you and your plumber.
3.
GROUNDWOOD PAPER
PORTA POTTY EDITION
For the truly fearless.
SCAREDY KAT
WHY AM I HERE?
STINKY CHRONICLES
✓ Printed on Amazon's groundwood paper
✓ Budget-friendly
✓ Lightweight & durable
✓ Inspired by every truck stop, campground, and roadside restroom in America
WARNING:
Reading this edition may cause spontaneous cackling from neighboring stalls.
The author accepts no responsibility for awkward eye contact through the porta potty door.
DUCK APPROVED
ONE AUTHOR. THREE EDITIONS.
COUNTLESS REGRETS.
SCAREDY KAT
Stories to Scare the Out of You!

SCAREDY KAT

STORIES TO SCARE THE 💩 OUT OF YOU!

THREE EDITIONS. THREE WAYS TO GET SCARED.

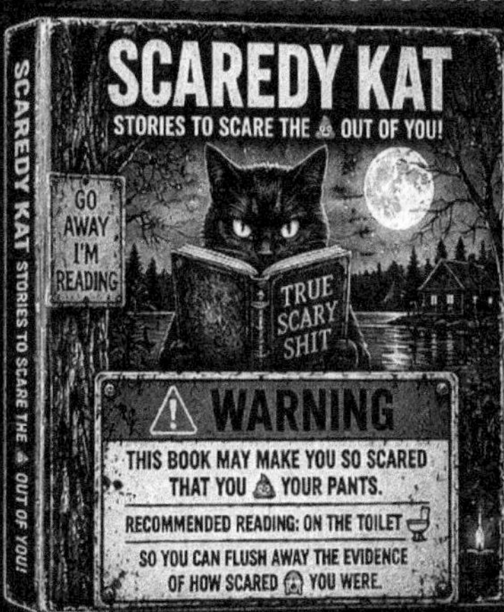

1 COLOR COLLECTOR'S EDITION

The complete Scaredy Kat experience in full, terrifying color. Every creepy detail brought to life.

FOR TRUE HORROR FANS.

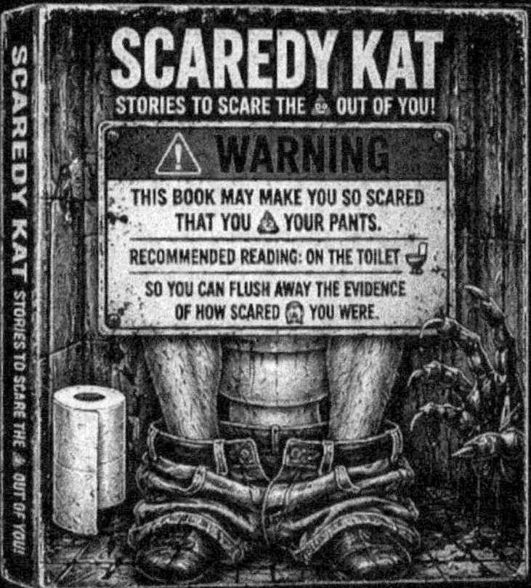

2 BLACK & WHITE TOILET EDITION

Stripped down. No distractions. Just you, your bathroom, and your worst fears.

FOR READERS WHO BELIEVE EVERY GREAT BOOK BELONGS IN A BATHROOM.

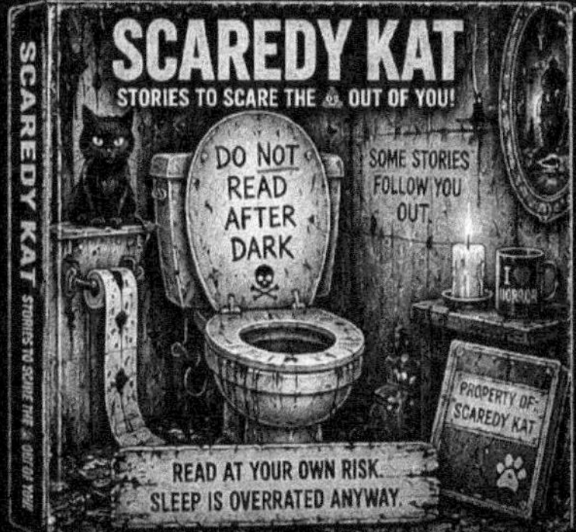

3 GROUNDWOOD PAPER PORTA POTTY EDITION

Printed on rustic groundwood paper for the ultimate backwoods horror experience.

 **ONE BOOK. THREE EDITIONS. COUNTLESS REGRETS.** 

SEQUEL TO SCAREDY KAT

THE SHITHEADS

THREE EDITIONS. CHOOSE YOUR DOOM.

- Premium full-color interior pages.
- Every horrifying detail.
- Maximum laughs, maximum trauma.
- Looks great on any bookshelf.

2 BLACK & WHITE TOILET EDITION

- Black & white interior pages.
- Same colorful cover you love.

3 GROUNDWOOD PAPER PORTA POTTY EDITION

- Printed on Amazon's groundwood paper.
- Budget-friendly.
- Lightweight & durable.
- Inspired by every truck stop, campground, and roadside restroom in America.

ONE BOOK. THREE EDITIONS. COUNTLESS REGRETS.

WARNING

Copyright © 2026 by Kat Smith
All rights reserved.

Fiction Disclaimer:

This is a work of humor and satire inspired by real-life situations. Names, characters, businesses, places, and events have been changed or fictionalized. Any resemblance to actual persons, living or dead, or real events is purely coincidental.

Published by:
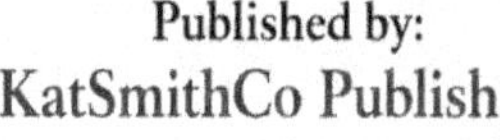
KatSmithCo Publishing
Southern California, USA

ISBN (Paperback – COLOR):
979-8-9957227-0-0
ISBN (Hardcover – COLOR):
979-8-9957227-1-7
ISBN (Paperback – Black & White):
979-8-9957227-2-4
ISBN (Hardcover – Black & White):
979-8-9957227-3-1
ISBN (Paperback – GROUNDWOOD):
979-8-950874-03-1
ISBN (Hardcover – GROUNDWOOD):
979-8-950874-02-4

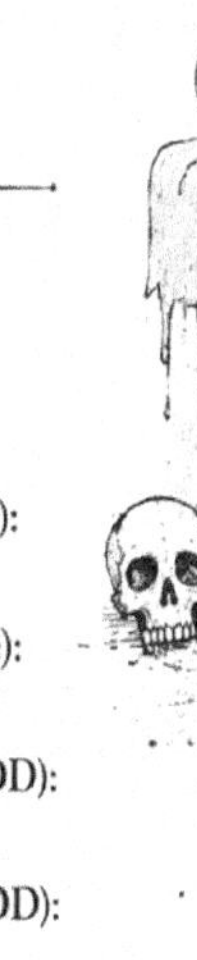

Cover Design & Interior Layout: Kat Smith
Author Photos & Creative Direction: Kat Smith

Trademark Notice:
"Scaredy Kat™" and all related titles, phrases, and branding are trademarks of KatSmithCo Publishing. Unauthorized use is prohibited.

First Edition
Printed in the United States of America

Because let's be honest...
Sometimes life gets shitty.

www.ingramcontent.com/pod-product-compliance
Lightning Source LLC
LaVergne TN
LVHW020705110826
845149LV00012B/2108
* 9 7 9 8 9 9 5 7 2 2 7 2 4 *